AN IMPOSSIBLE LOVE

France, 1943: Aliénor Rochefontaine de Montfort, only child of impoverished aristocratic parents, works for the Resistance. She nurses Peter Maybury back to health, a British agent badly injured while operating behind enemy lines — and falls in love with him. But her parents have already arranged her marriage to Henri d'Eparnelle, whose wealth will restore her family's fortunes. Torn between duty to her family and love for the man who means the world to her, Aliénor faces an impossible choice.

KATE FINNEMORE

◆

AN IMPOSSIBLE LOVE

Complete and Unabridged

LINFORD
Leicester

First published in Great Britain in 2017

First Linford Edition
published 2019

A catalogue record for this book is available
from the British Library.

ISBN 978–1–4448–4005–6

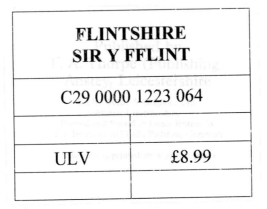

1

The alarms went off in the early hours. Aliénor woke to the sounds of shouted orders, the pounding of booted feet on gravel and the roar of engines as German jeeps sped away. Exultation sparked through her. Anything that disrupted the Nazis' normal activities was a plus, a small victory for France.

The Germans had requisitioned the north wing of her parents' château three years before, in June 1940 when they'd invaded France. The sights and sounds of the three officers, their men and a variety of military vehicles had long since become familiar. She still couldn't accept their presence, though.

Straight after breakfast, she cycled into the village and found German soldiers stopping everyone and checking their papers. As she got down off her bicycle and stood in the short, nervous queue, she saw Captain Ralf Horelbeck, one of the three officers billeted at the château. Tall, in his mid-twenties, and good-looking despite the uniform he wore, he stood on the far side of the checkpoint, studying the features of each person that passed it. Glancing her way, he gave an almost imperceptible nod of recognition.

The last few days had been hot and sunny, but now the temperature was building, and the air had become thick and heavy. A fitful wind gusted, kicking up swirls of dust from the dry roadway, and Aliénor shivered. In spite of the captain's presence, she was apprehensive.

'What's going on, Ralf?' she asked the captain when, to her relief, she passed the checkpoint without a problem. Beyond him she could see people coming together in fluid groups, darting quick anxious glances at the soldiers who seemed to be everywhere. Almost immediately they would re-form, disappear into the café, reappear. The muted buzz of excited voices filled the air. Whatever had happened was almost certainly good news, and Aliénor felt a thrill speed through her.

'I'm afraid I can't tell you that, *mademoiselle*.' Both tone and words were a rebuff, and Aliénor's cheeks grew warm. The German captain relaxed his posture a fraction. 'Aliénor . . . ' he began. Lifting his hand as if to touch her arm, he thought better of it perhaps, and let it drop back down to his side. '*Bonne journée, mademoiselle*.'

Aliénor walked on, pushing her bicycle, rerunning that odd little episode through her mind. She joined the first group she came to, and her thoughts were instantly taken in a different direction.

'Have you heard the news, *mademoiselle* Aliénor?'

'Saboteurs have blown up the railway line — '

'Just north of here — '

'The explosion tipped the loco on its side — '

'The Morelle boy saw it with his own eyes.'

All too aware of the German presence only metres away, they kept their voices low. But their words fizzed with excitement, the gestures that accompanied them rapid and animated. Aliénor's hand came up to cover her mouth. It was amazing news. Unbelievable news. A broad smile spread over her face. All at once her feet itched to move: she wanted to dance with joy.

'They haven't caught them.' The speaker, the young primary school teacher in her first year of teaching, cast a fearful glance at the soldiers by the checkpoint.

'Yet.'

'That's why the Germans are out in force.'

The group fell silent, following with their eyes as two soldiers, rifles slung on their shoulders, marched past them. Aliénor suppressed a shiver.

'Have the Germans told you what they're going to do next, *mademoiselle*

4

Aliénor?' asked the blacksmith.

She gave a bitter laugh. 'You know they rarely tell us anything, André.'

'What about the young captain, *mademoiselle*?' asked the café-owner's wife, nodding towards Ralf.

Aliénor shook her head. 'He's saying nothing either.' She looked across at him. His expression was grim, and unease whispered down her spine.

She wasn't alone in feeling uneasy. As she moved from group to group, she was aware of the gradual darkening of the mood. Rumours sprang up as fact was mixed with speculation. There were German checkpoints on all the roads out of the village. The Gestapo were coming. There would be reprisals. In the nearby town of Loudun, ten men had been taken and shot — or would be taken and shot, depending on who she listened to. She saw faces become shuttered and heard the anxiety as people dropped their voices to a hushed undertone.

Tension crackled in the air. Aliénor

looked up at the sky. Storm clouds were massing in the south-west. Flurries of the gusting wind picked up dust and swirled it round, but failed to lighten the oppressive atmosphere. Thunder rumbled, far in the distance.

With a growing sense of urgency, Aliénor climbed back onto her bicycle. Common sense told her she should pay her visits in and around the village and return to the safety of the château as fast as possible.

⋆ ⋆ ⋆

It was not yet noon when Aliénor cycled down the narrow lane bordered on both sides by high stone walls which led to her final destination, the isolated farmhouse where Suzanne Moulis and her young son Jérôme lived. Aged eighteen and the only child of Vincent and Thérèse Rochefontaine de Mont-fort, Aliénor was already taking over some of her mother's duties on the estate.

The storm was still far away, the thunder a deep murmur. Though the breeze made by the movement of her bicycle gave an illusion of coolness, her blouse was sticking to her back.

The double gates and side door that led to Suzanne's farmhouse were closed, and Aliénor's stomach lurched as she remembered the last time she'd found them shut. She jumped down from her bicycle and propped it against the wall.

'Suzanne,' she called, rapping on the side door.

A clatter of clogs. A panted, urgent, 'Who is it?'

'Aliénor.'

The door opened and she gasped with shock. Suzanne's hair was lank and straggly, her face pale and shiny with sweat. But relief at seeing Aliénor relaxed the taut lines. 'You're early. Thank goodness. Come on in. Please.' The words spilled out.

'What is it, Suzanne? Is it the baby? Is it on its way?' Aliénor stepped through the side door into the court-yard and put her arm round the other woman. The edges of the faded wraparound apron Suzanne wore no longer met across her bulging stomach. The baby was due any day. From the corner of her eye she saw young Jérôme hiding in the shadows of the open doorway to the kitchen.

'No.' But a look of surprise crossed her face and she bent forward, both hands cupping her belly. 'I'm fine. Aunt Apolline'll be here soon, anyway.' No relation to Suzanne, Aunt Apolline was the village wise woman. Now that Suzanne was near her term, Aliénor had arranged for her to cycle over to the isolated farmhouse every day.

'Good.' She rubbed the other woman's shoulder reassuringly.

'It's Christian.' Like Aliénor, Suzanne called her cousin only by his codename now. 'He wants you up there. At the hut. You've got to go up there straight away.'

A hollow fear lodged in Aliénor's

chest. She and Christian met often so that she could pass on all she knew about the movements and intentions of the Germans at the château. But today wasn't the day they had decided on for their next meeting. 'He came here himself? It wasn't someone else who came here with the message?'

'Yes. No.' There was an edge of panic in Suzanne's voice. 'It was Christian. This morning. He wants you to take some things with you. It's urgent. Very urgent.' She grimaced as a fresh spasm took her. 'Come inside. Please.'

Anxiety sent a chill across Aliénor's skin. In the three months since she'd met Christian, she'd grown to like and respect him. He was steady and reliable, and didn't exaggerate. If he said something was urgent, he meant exactly that.

Clouds had covered the midday sun so that even less light than normal entered the large kitchen. The smell of wood smoke and soot filled the room. A pot hung from a hook above the log fire that burned in the grate. Water bubbled up from under the lid and fell sizzling on to the dull-glowing embers. Aliénor thought she caught the starchy smell of potatoes.

'Can you help me with these? Please.' Suzanne moved heavily over to the table, picking up a knife and the corner of a linen sheet. With a brisk upward movement of the knife, she cut into the edge of the sheet and ripped the strip off all along its length, sending a cloud of white dust up into the air.

'Here, give me that. You sit down.' Gripped by the same sense of urgency, Aliénor took the knife and the sheet from her. The material was thick and coarsely woven, and had a musty smell about it as if it had only that morning been brought out of storage. About a dozen lengths already lay in a tumbled heap on the table. Suzanne sat, picked up one of the strips and started rolling it up.

'Bandages?' Aliénor frowned, puzzled thoughts racing as she stood on the other side of the table, and cut and ripped the sheet. She looked across at Suzanne. 'These aren't for you. You don't need bandages. And they're not for Christian. He came here this morning, you said? So you could have bandaged him here if he'd needed it. Oh!'

The air whooshed out of her lungs. So that was it. Aliénor felt herself go pale with the shock of it. The knife dropped with a clatter to the table. She reached out blindly for the chair beside her and sank down into it, still holding the thin strip of bandage in one hand, the linen sheet in the other.

She looked at Suzanne. 'It's the man, one of the men, who blew up the railway line, isn't it?' She spoke as much to herself as to the other woman. She was in no doubt she had hit on the truth. All at once she was almost too frightened to breathe. It was as if a yawning chasm had opened beneath her feet, and she was falling, falling, plunging into danger. All the Germans

11

in the area would be looking for this man. And hadn't someone said the Gestapo were coming?

Suzanne stared back at her. 'I don't know. I don't know what you're talking about. Christian told me nothing.' The edge of panic in her voice was stronger now. 'But we've got to get a move on. Christian said it's urgent.'

Aliénor's mind went blank. Then her thoughts skittered off in all directions. Hospital. They'd have to get him to a hospital. The nearest one was in Loudun. No. That'd be the first place the Germans would go. A doctor? There were two in Loudun. No, three. But she wasn't sure where their sympathies lay. It'd depend where he was hurt. How had they got him up to the hut? Who got him up there? Him? It could be a woman. It might be a bullet wound. Yarrow worked wonders for things like that, didn't it? Was it the right time of year for yarrow?

A crack of thunder, close and loud, made Aliénor jump. She saw Suzanne watching her, and stood up. This was no good. She had to think straight. Above all she had to reassure the woman sitting opposite her. With the baby on its way, Suzanne already had enough to worry about.

'Forget what I said, Suzanne. Just something I heard in the village.' It was an effort to sound so calm. She looked over at Jérôme, stock-still in the doorway, his face pale and pinched, and wondered how much Suzanne's son had heard. It was dangerous, even for a five-year-old, to know too much. She gestured at the tumble of linen on the table. 'We don't need to roll these. Much quicker just to fold them.'

Flinching as another contraction caught her, Suzanne reached across, took first one strip, then another, folding them with deft fingers.

'Did Christian say anything else — anything else I need to bring?'

'Medicine and soap. But I haven't got either.'

Medicine and soap. Apprehension

13

uncoiled deep in Aliénor's stomach. What was she going to find up there? And did she have the strength to deal with it?

2

Thunder crashed overhead, rolling round and round, again and again, in a long echoing rumble as Aliénor approached the grape-pickers' hut, the remote hideaway where she reported to her Resistance contact, Suzanne's cousin Christian.

She slid off her bicycle and pushed it and herself into the safety of the ferns and trees on her left, cuffing the sweat from her forehead. A faint trembling shook her whole body. She'd driven herself hard to get here before the storm broke, and that explained in part her rapidly beating heart and shaking body. But the main cause, she knew, was a growing apprehension and a fear deeper-seated than anything she'd experienced before.

She flexed her hands and wrists, easing the blood flow back into them, and looked across at the hut. No smoke came from the chimney. Standing some fifty metres away in one corner of the overgrown vineyard and covered at the front by thick brambles, the stone-built hut looked abandoned. But Aliénor stayed where she was, without moving, eyes and ears alert to danger.

She and Christian both took great care in their comings and goings, and she was as certain as she could be that the hideaway remained undiscovered. But there was always the possibility that the Germans *did* know of its existence and had set a trap for her or for Christian, or for both.

The sweet scent of the yarrow she'd picked on her way up to the hut mingled with the musty smell of the linen that lay folded underneath it in the basket on her handlebars. Suzanne had also put a couple of candles and a dish of potatoes in the basket, neither of which she could really spare, Aliénor knew. It was bad luck to wish someone 'good luck' so she and Suzanne had come together in a long, wordless hug. Aliénor had felt the fine quiver in the other woman's body and recognised without surprise that she too was scared. For their different reasons, both of them feared what the immediate future would bring.

Lightning zigzagged across the sky, an eerie backlight to the low clouds. Thunder boomed. The storm was directly above, frightening in its intensity. But she had seen, heard or smelt nothing else to alarm her, and it was high time she left the safety of the woods. Hunching her shoulders, Aliénor pushed her bicycle out of the undergrowth and headed at a run towards the hut just as fat raindrops began to fall. Few in number for the moment, they bounced up off the dry path in a cloud of dust.

Christian had rigged up a screen of ivy round at the rear of the hut. As Aliénor hid her bicycle behind it, she touched the handlebars of his and her fingers came away sticky with something dark. She stood there motionless, thoughts swirling, before straightening her spine, grimly resolute.

Lifting her basket from the handlebars she moved swiftly to the door and rapped out four regular beats.

'Who is it?'

Low and cautious, but it was Christian's voice. Aliénor's relief was enormous. 'Mélisande,' she said, using her codename.

She bent her head to enter the hut and recoiled as the sharp metallic smell of blood hit her. She glanced in wide-eyed shock at Christian and held on to the door, preventing him from closing it behind her.

'We're going to need some light in here,' she said as her gaze went to the figure who lay, partly shrouded by a blanket, on the makeshift bed along the far wall. 'And some air.' Her voice was an urgent whisper. The single room of the hut was hot and dark and full of shadows. The light that now came in from outside helped, but only a little. The man's eyes were shut, she could see, as if he were asleep, but he moved constantly, restlessly. With a grimace he would draw his left leg up to his chest and let it fall back down again to the bed. Fingers of both hands were taut, splayed out, and hovered quivering, wanting to touch the leg but not daring to, it seemed. His face too worked constantly, creasing as though he were in great pain. But no sound came from his mouth.

With a cry she sank to her knees beside the man, setting her basket with its precious load of herbs and bandages down on the earth floor next to her. In the gloomy light she could see a darker pool of something that had seeped into the fabric, a blanket or coat, that served as a pillow. Her fingers reached out but stayed poised, not touching. The smell of blood was strong and pervasive, and Aliénor's stomach turned. Lightning flashed, and in its glare she saw his face and hands were pocked by cuts, black against the unearthly white of his skin. Some glistened with blood, others thankfully were dry.

Christian squatted beside her and she opened her mouth to speak, but the words wouldn't come.

'I've done what I could for his face and hands.' Christian's voice was ragged with tiredness. His eyes behind the round lenses of his glasses were dark shadows. 'Bits of metal and stone had gone into the flesh. I've dug out all the bits I could see. But it's his leg I'm worried about.'

Aliénor swallowed hard and ran her tongue round the inside of her mouth. Despite the limited resources at his disposal, he appeared to have made a good job of it. 'We'll need water. Clean water.' Her voice was small and scared. She wasn't up to this task. She couldn't help this man. She knew it. 'We've got to boil the water. We'll have to risk a fire. No one'll see the smoke in this weather.'

'I'll see to it right away.'

'Your shirt,' she gasped, not understanding, when Christian stood up. 'What's happened to your shirt?' He wore a grey heavy-duty cotton shirt. Open at the neck, tucked in at his waistband and with the sleeves rolled up, from the front it looked perfectly normal. But as he turned away from her, she could see that the portion of cloth at the back between the two side seams and the yoke was missing, leaving his bare back visible.

Christian nodded towards the injured man. 'You'll see.'

Slowly, reluctantly, afraid of what she'd find, Aliénor turned to the man on the bed. The rain had picked up, and drummed hard on the slate roof of the hut. The thunder and lightning were constant now, an unrestrained confusion of noise and light. Behind her, she could just about hear Christian at the fireplace. A faint scent of wood smoke told her he'd managed to light the kindling with his flint. The water from the spring was clear and pure, but dregs

21

of wine in the bottles he used to bring it to the hut might well contaminate it.

Squaring her shoulders, steeling herself, Aliénor moved the coarse woollen blanket down. The man wore a black jersey and trousers. The left leg of the trousers had been ripped open along the seam, the fabric pushed up and a strip of grey cloth, part of Christian's shirt no doubt, had been knotted round the man's thigh just above the knee.

Aliénor drew the blanket down further and sucked in a shocked breath. The rest of Christian's shirt had been torn into strips and wrapped round the man's leg from knee to ankle. She didn't know how long the improvised bandage had been in place, but it was soaked in blood now.

She bent forward, using the tips of shaking fingers to undo the knot that kept the bandage in place. The man flinched, tried to edge his leg away. She darted a look at his face and saw rather than heard the pain that hissed through his teeth. His eyes were screwed tight shut. Taking care not to touch the wound, she found herself wincing as she eased the cloth away. Briefly she closed her eyes, in a vain attempt to blot out the awful sight.

The leg below the knee was a mess of raw flesh. Skin and muscle. White tendons, and dark blood welling. The man must be in agony, yet not one sound had escaped his lips. Sickness rose in her throat. She shook her head, inching away on her knees from the injured man. Her mind, her whole body, shrank from the task that faced her. What could she do? She wasn't a nurse. She couldn't help this man, she thought, the beginnings of panic setting in.

Christian's hand on her shoulder steadied her. 'It was the explosion.' A crack of thunder boomed in echo to his words. The rain beat down even harder on the roof. 'Part of the rail got thrown up and ripped through his leg.'

So she'd guessed right, back at

Suzanne's farmhouse. This was the man who had sabotaged the railway line north of Loudun. Aliénor's gaze swept from the long wound in his leg to his battered hands and face, and her heart swelled with a mixture of respect and awe.

'I must wash my hands.' She scrambled to her feet. Rolling up the sleeves of her blouse, she made her way to the open door of the hut. There, she held her hands out, letting the rainwater stream over them. She used the thumbnail of one hand to clean beneath the nails of the other, and shook both hands dry. What she would give for carbolic soap. Rainwater was nothing more than a poor second-best. Perhaps it would be better to do nothing. No. She rejected the thought straight away. The man was suffering right now. She had to try and do something. She had to be strong.

Christian had poured water from the pot on the fire into an enamel dish on the mantelpiece. Aliénor dipped her finger in and out.

'Perfect,' she said. An unnatural calm had come over her. She crossed the room and knelt beside the bed again, putting the dish by her basket and handing Christian one of Suzanne's candles. 'Can you light this, Christian, please?'

Waiting until he had set it on the shelf above the bed, she tore off a piece of one of the linen bandages, moistened it in the water and dabbed gently at one edge of the long jagged injury. The man's reaction was instant. He recoiled, his face contorting, like a soul in torment. His head came up, his eyes snapping open, his hands pushing at hers. His gaze, dark and unfathomable, met hers.

'I'm sorry,' she whispered. She was close to tears. It was almost impossible to stay calm. But she knew she had to. This man's life might depend on it. 'Here, take this.' She reached into her basket and fetched out one of the stalks of yarrow. Pulling the leaves off, she broke part of the stem into several short pieces and pushed them into the man's mouth. 'Chew it. Go on.' She watched as he flopped back on to the pillow, eyes closed, mouth slowly chewing. 'Yarrow,' she said to Christian. 'It'll help kill the pain.'

'I know. My father always had some on him in the last war. Kept it in his first aid kit.' Her presence had given Christian a new lease of life, Aliénor thought, but his hands trembled, and she knew he was close to the end of his tether.

'Mine did too.' She bent over the man's leg again, cleaning the injury as delicately as she could. 'He said it saved his life once. At Verdun.'

To Aliénor's relief, the man lay still, his eyes now open, now closed. Only his mouth moved as he chewed the yarrow as if it were a wad of tobacco. But his hands, at his sides, were clenched into fists and Aliénor knew his stillness wasn't so much the effect of the plant as the result of an iron self-control. The same iron self-control that stopped him shouting out his pain.

'So tell me what happened,' she said to Christian. In the flickering light of the candle, she used a corner of the linen to draw out a shred of fabric. Sickly, she wondered how many other such shreds she'd be leaving behind to rot and turn the wound septic.

'He was showing us how to lay explosives. That's why he's here.' The thunder was now a distant rumble, the lightning an occasional flash. In the comparative calm, Aliénor was conscious of a growing confidence as she and Christian fell into a regular rhythm. While he tended the fire, prepared the yarrow, and refilled the dish with newly boiled water, Aliénor cleaned a section of the wound, closed the edges as best she could, laid feathery yarrow leaves across to staunch the bleeding, and wrapped a bandage around that part of the man's leg. Starting at his ankle, she gradually worked her way along the jagged mess.

'Everything was in place,' Christian went on. 'The explosive, the fuse, the time pencil. A ten-minute one. But fifteen minutes went by and nothing had happened. It was a dud, he thought. We heard the train stop at the station about a kilometre up the track, and knew it'd be along in a quarter of an hour or so. There was no time to lose. So he went up close to the rail. He was going to fix another pencil in place. And that's when it happened. The first one wasn't a dud after all.'

He fell silent, remembering, and Aliénor didn't interrupt.

'Getting him back here was a nightmare,' he continued some while later. 'We had to get away from the railway line before the Germans got there. So the other two helped me bandage his leg up as best we could, and between us we managed to get him up on my bike. We set off in three different directions. Less chance of *all* of us getting caught that way.' He crossed over from the fireplace with a fresh dish of boiled water. 'And I just pushed and pushed him and that bloody bike until we got here. The sun had been up for a couple of hours at least by then.'

It was the first time Aliénor had heard this thoughtful, bookish man swear. She twisted round, reaching up, touching her fingers to his wrist. 'You poor thing.'

'And all for an operation that failed miserably,' he added bitterly, crouching beside her.

'But it didn't! One of the village boys said he saw a locomotive over on its side.'

'He did?' A sudden wondering smile lit his face, chasing away his tiredness, for the moment at least. 'The train driver can't have seen the gap in the line.'

'Or maybe he did see it, and drove the loco over it anyway.' Aliénor's eyes met his. Both knew there was an increasing number of railway workers complicit in acts of sabotage. 'Pass me a few more leaves of yarrow, will you.' She'd almost finished dressing the leg wound, and would tackle the man's hands next. She thought he'd fallen asleep at last. The rain had finally stopped, and it was a little cooler in the hut.

Aliénor paused, considering. 'I suppose you could say he was lucky only his face, hands and just the one leg got hurt. It could have been much worse.'

Christian nodded towards the fabric folded to form a pillow under the man's head. 'His coat protected him. Thank God he was wearing it.'

'Has he got a name?' she asked, laying the soft leaves across the injury. She meant codename of course.

'Weyland,' Christian answered, stumbling over the 'w'.

Aliénor frowned. 'That's a strange one. Does it mean anything?'

Christian shrugged. 'No idea.'

There was something deep in the flesh. Aliénor probed with the strip of cloth, folded into a point, knowing she had to get it out.

'Jesus,' the man hissed, jerking his knee up and away.

It was a single word. But it was like a jolt of electricity shooting through her. 'Oh!' Aliénor rocked back on her heels. Her eyes, wide with the shock of it, flew to Christian. He looked away, a fraction too late. He knew!

'You could have told me.' She spoke in a harsh whisper, each syllable clipped with suppressed anger.

'Would it have made any difference?' Christian countered quietly.

She held his gaze a second or two longer before shaking her head, anger seeping away. The answer, of course, was 'no'. She turned back to the man on the bed. For one long moment, his dark eyes watched her, tense and still.

Her mind was whirling. A hospital was out of the question now. That much was clear. A doctor too, out of the question. She clenched her hands as a fresh spurt of anger gripped her. The man was condemned to live — or, more likely, die — by her own amateurish efforts.

That single word had given him away. It was the same word in her own language. But his pronunciation and intonation were unmistakable. Fear prickled down her back. She looked from one man to the other. Now she understood why his strange codename didn't sound at all French.

The man was English.

3

Flinching from the pain of it, each movement an agony, the man with the foreign-sounding codename levered himself onto his right elbow.

'No, don't,' Aliénor cried. 'You'll start the bleeding up again. Don't get up. You're safe here. You're with friends.' She reached forward to push him back down onto the bed, and gasped when his fingers curled round her wrist, stopping her. His hand was cut and scabbed, and rough on her skin.

'She's one of us.' Christian was at her side still, a reassuring presence, his anxiety barely perceptible beneath his soothing tone, and the man's grip round her wrist relaxed a fraction. He spat out what remained of the yarrow stalk.

'Christian, put the fire out.' He spoke

French now, good French, but his voice struggled with the effort of talking. 'The rain's stopped. If the *Boches* see the smoke, they'll be crawling all over the place in no time at all.' He had a slight accent, but few Germans would be able to detect it, Aliénor thought. His eyes, dark-shadowed by tiredness and pain, settled on her face. 'Leave that cut alone. You've done enough. I'll take my chances.'

'No.' Aliénor shook her head. 'There's something in there. I've got to get it out.'

Their eyes met. A flash of lightning flared, and Aliénor could see the taut, dangerous lines of his face. People usually did what this man said, she sensed with a shiver. Even now, she could hear Christian by the fireplace doing as the man had asked, kicking and treading on the glowing embers of the fire.

The man's grip round her wrist loosened, his long fingers skimming up and down her forearm in a touch so feather-light that a tremor rippled along her skin.

'I didn't mean to sound ungrateful,' he said. 'I can never thank you and Christian enough for what you've done.' Thunder rumbled far in the distance, and she saw him brace himself. 'Go on. Do it,' he growled, his hand dropping from her arm back to the bed.

For a second Aliénor couldn't move. With a sound that was almost a sob, she picked a fresh strip of linen from her basket, folded it into a point and dipped it into the dish of water Christian set down beside her.

If it had been bad before, it was worse now. Then, he'd slipped in and out of sleep, in and out of consciousness as he lay in the stifling, airless hut. Now he was fully awake, and forced to endure every dig and prod and probe. His hands hovered either side of hers, crisping, uncurling, and Aliénor was wretchedly aware she was putting him through agony. Yet throughout it all, he kept his leg perfectly still, and she could only wonder at his courage.

A long gruelling minute later, she slid a tiny square of fabric glistening with blood out of the wound.

'Not long now.' She felt sick.

'Thank Christ for that.'

It was spoken with feeling. Aliénor wiped her hand across her forehead and looked up. The light from outside was stronger now, chasing away the shadows made by the flickering candle, and for the first time she was able to see him properly.

Dark lashes and arching eyebrows, the day's growth of beard and the cuts now scabbing over stood out starkly against the pallor of his skin. It was the face of a man whose role here in France kept him close to the shadows of the night, Aliénor thought with a shudder. She put him in his mid-twenties. Too young, surely, to be dicing with death in what was for him a foreign land.

His hair was thick and unruly, and

gleamed damply with sweat or blood, recalling Aliénor to her task. Easing her legs, cramped from what seemed like hours of kneeling, she started again.

At last it was over. She'd dressed the injuries on his hands and the large gash on the back of his head, and he lay there now, eyes closed. She sat back on her heels, massaging the small of her back with her fist. Her eyes were dry and scratchy from tiredness and concentration. She was drained physically and emotionally. All she wanted was to get back home and sleep for a thousand years.

Aliénor got to her feet, easing her stiff shoulders, moving her numb legs on the spot. She ran her fingers like a comb through her hair. Her skin was sticky with sweat. She looked down at herself, examining her sleeves and the front of her blouse and skirt, and her shoulders slumped with relief. The fabric of both was crumpled but there were no obvious bloodstains. Would she pass muster, though, if she ran into a German patrol?

She went over to Christian, who stood by the fireplace. 'You look all in,' she said, kissing him on both cheeks. 'You need to get some sleep.'

She turned, intending to pick up her basket, and saw that the Englishman had opened his eyes and was watching her. On the spur of the moment, she crossed to the bed and knelt beside him.

'Don't move,' she said, and kissed him too on both cheeks.

The flat of his hand, rough with bandages, touched her arm, staying her. 'Will you be coming back?' His voice was husky with pain.

Aliénor's gaze moved over his features. How she ached for him. This man had been unbelievably brave — and he would need all that courage time and again in the days to come. 'Yes. Tomorrow. I'll come back tomorrow. If I can.'

'Good.' A fleeting smile relaxed his

face, and he closed his eyes again, his hand sliding down her arm and back on to the bed.

She stayed where she was, looking at him, suddenly breathless. Standing up quickly, she leaned over him to blow out the candle before stooping to pick up her basket.

'I must go, Christian,' she said, putting what was left of the yarrow and bandages on the mantelpiece. All at once her voice was as husky as the Englishman's.

★   ★   ★

It was as if the land had been reborn. No trace of the storm remained. High in the sky shreds of cloud were blown along by the wind, but here at ground level there was just a light breeze. Aliénor stood outside the grape-pickers' hut, relishing the warmth of the afternoon sun on her face and arms. The air was fresh and clear, with none of the oppression of the morning.

Wildflowers, vines, the leaves of trees all sparkled in the sunlight, so bright it hurt the eyes. After the hell of the hut and the injured man it held, this was heaven.

Aliénor looked at her watch. Almost four. She wouldn't go through the village, she decided, pulling her bicycle out from its hiding place behind the screen of ivy and fixing the basket in place. Better to keep to back roads and tracks. About to climb on and cycle off, she paused, recalling with a faint frown that odd little moment of breathlessness. The Englishman's bravery had clearly affected her deeply.

The calm aftermath of the storm had brought people out. As she cycled along, Aliénor waved to those she saw working in the fields — mainly women and old men of course; the Germans had taken most of the young men away — or called a greeting to others who simply sat soaking up the sun outside their houses. Gradually her tiredness slipped from her shoulders. But the fear that had been a constant backdrop to the day was still there, lodged like a cancer deep inside.

It was just before five when she wheeled her bicycle round past the south wing of the château. Only too aware that her clothes were creased and not very clean, her hair uncombed, she wanted to put her bicycle away, go to her room, and wash and change before anyone, especially her keen-eyed mother, could see her and ask awkward questions.

'So here you are at last, Aliénor.'

Her heart sank. She spun round to see her mother looking down at her from the terrace that ran all along the back of the château.

'Go put on your prettiest dress. The one with the sprigs of pink flowers on it, perhaps. We've got special guests joining us this evening. The Gestapo. They came down from Paris earlier today.' Her mother's tone was neutral. It was impossible to know what she was really thinking.

41

She was well aware that her parents collaborated with the enemy. Because they had no choice? Or were they willing collaborators? It wasn't something she and her mother had ever discussed. They didn't have that kind of relationship. The answer to her question, Aliénor sensed uneasily, was that her mother would do whatever was in the Rochefontaine de Montfort's best interests.

An hour later Aliénor stood, the first to arrive, in one corner of the terrace, self-conscious in the dress her mother had decided on. She was too tall, all arms and legs, and long feet and hands, an awkward gangling eighteen-year-old. She was tense too, afraid of somehow giving away what she knew about the men who'd blown the railway line up.

The sound of footsteps on the flagstones made her turn.

'Captain Ralf Horelbeck at your service, *mademoiselle*.' The German officer clicked his heels and bowed his head, his arms held stiffly at his sides.

Like the other two officers billeted at the château, he spoke good French.

Aliénor laughed, though a part of her remained wary, as always. He *was* the enemy, after all. 'Don't be silly, Ralf!'

He grinned. 'I'm getting into practice for the bigwigs.'

'*Mère* said we had some special guests coming. The Gestapo. Who exactly?'

Ralf didn't reply. He looked past her and Aliénor turned to see her parents approaching, arm in arm. Her mother always wore shades of mauve. Tonight she glittered in a pale lilac gown studded with sequins, while Aliénor's father wore his habitual three-piece suit, dark grey this time.

'Captain Horelbeck, evening. The storm's cleared the air, I see.' Vincent Rochefontaine de Montfort was already turning away. He never lingered long with the junior ranks. 'Come, Thérèse. Our guests have arrived.'

With a practised eye, Thérèse looked her daughter up and down and gave a nod of approval.

With Ralf at her side, Aliénor followed her parents, crossing the terrace to greet the new arrivals. General Friedrich Hartmann, the most senior of the officers billeted at the château, carried out the introductions. Théodore Gaillard, in his early forties, Aliénor judged, was the deputy director of Radio-Paris, the radio station that broadcast news and music throughout France and beyond. He shook hands with each person present, clasping their hand warmly in both his. French, and a more-than-willing collaborator, Aliénor thought with disgust, hard put to hide her contempt for the man as she in turn shook his hand.

His companion, tall, pale and very blond, was a different matter entirely. Dressed in the grey uniform of the Gestapo, he looked to be in his mid- to late thirties, and was introduced to them as Colonel Ernst Ostermeyer, the acting director of the French Propaganda Department.

'Just filling in while Colonel Schmidtke is on sick leave,' General Hartmann explained. Normally a confident, coolly efficient soldier, even he appeared to Aliénor to be wary of the newcomer who, unsmiling, clicked his heels together and briefly bowed his head. It was a token gesture of greeting, almost an insult.

A maid approached holding a tray of glasses filled with red wine.

'Just our local stuff, I'm afraid,' Aliénor's father said. There was a short uncomfortable silence. Aliénor held her breath, knowing he'd made the remark deliberately, reminding everyone that the Germans had shipped all the good wine back to Germany. 'Would you like to try some, Colonel Ostermeyer?' He indicated the tray of glasses.

'Yes, of course,' the German replied. His tone was smooth and revealed nothing. He took a glass and with no further word turned his back on them to survey the grounds of the château and the lake in the distance. The three officers looked at each other before taking a glass each and reforming into a tight-knit group a few feet away.

Aliénor stayed with her parents, who engaged the deputy director of Radio-Paris in conversation. When Théodore Gaillard offered her a cigarette from the silver case he took out of his pocket, she accepted, hiding her dislike at the way he leant close to her to light it. His dark slicked-back hair held the sickly smell of Parma violets.

She sipped at her wine and let the talk wash over her. The scent of honeysuckle reached her through the still evening air. From time to time the hum of conversation on the terrace was punctuated by shouted commands and the revving of engines from the north wing of the château. The ordinary soldiers and, Aliénor supposed, lower ranks of the Gestapo were busy. Her hands clenched and her thoughts went to the remote hut where Christian and the Englishman hid. They hadn't been found yet, she reasoned. If they had,

Colonel Ostermeyer wouldn't be here. He'd be interrogating them.

The colonel still stood with his back to the gathering, his hands clasped behind him. Aliénor drew in a shaky breath as she recalled the Englishman's touch on her arm. How was he faring? she wondered, and her heart gave a little leap.

'One small act of sabotage during the night,' Théodore Gaillard was saying. 'Even as I speak, the Gestapo are out looking for the perpetrators. We'll soon catch them, be in no doubt about it.' His eyes fell to Aliénor's breasts, gently rounded beneath the sweetheart neckline of the dress she wore. She stiffened. 'You must be glad, *mademoiselle*, that the war has passed you by in this quiet corner of France.'

Her hands clenched into fists. 'Glad as a caged bird is glad,' she muttered under her breath, forcing herself to stay calm. If she were provoked to anger, she might reveal too much. But how she'd have loved to tell him what she really thought, that they were prisoners in their own country, that his radio station was nothing but a propaganda machine for the Nazis, that she did all she could for the growing Resistance movement.

All at once, she became aware of the charged silence around her. Her words, quiet though they'd been, must have been overheard.

Her father shifted uneasily. 'I wouldn't go that far, Aliénor,' he said, an unmistakable warning in his tone.

Her mother's voice tinkled with light, false laughter. 'Why, it's not *that* quiet here, *monsieur*! We had six air raid alarms in Poitiers last month.' She shot a look at her daughter.

Colonel Ostermeyer turned round. His Aryan blue eyes, cold as ice, scoured her features. His face was hard, unforgiving. 'Caged, *mademoiselle*?'

She should have ignored the soft menace in his voice, should have apologised for speaking out of turn, and moved away. Instead she said, 'We're kept in the dark. We're never told — '

'Aliénor!' Her mother again. Another warning.

' — what's really going on.'

'My daughter is young, Colonel,' her mother cut in. 'And foolish.'

'And what *is* really going on, *mademoiselle?*'

She took a mouthful of her wine, had to fight to stop it going down the wrong way. In answer to his question she shook her head, angry with herself for taking the coward's way out and saying nothing.

His eyes flicked over her and she was aware of the keen, analytical intelligence behind them. He was no fool, she realised. She forced herself to meet his scrutiny as he dropped his cigarette and ground it out under his heel.

'There are times, *mademoiselle*, when it is more politic to keep silent.' He turned to Aliénor's father. 'Come, *monsieur*. You were going to give me a tour of the château. Are you joining us, Gaillard?'

She watched the three men walk

away. She was shaking.

'Aliénor.' Her mother joined her. Concealing her anger behind a bright smile, she said, 'That was disgraceful. You put us all in danger.' She walked off, leaving her daughter staring after her, mouth open in shock.

Major Kellner, the last of the three officers billeted at the château, brought a wind-up gramophone player out, set it down on a low table, and put a record on. Soon the haunting notes of a Dietrich song drifted through the evening air.

'Would *mademoiselle* care to dance?' It was Ralf.

Aliénor smiled a rueful smile. '*Mademoiselle* would.' She allowed herself to be taken into his arms. He was taller than her, and warm and strong, and she found herself relaxing a little as the shaking stopped. 'My God, Ralf, what was I thinking of? Why on earth didn't I keep my head down below the parapet? Just like everyone else around here,' she added bitterly. Not for the first time, she found herself speaking honestly with this man. In other circumstances, she knew, he could have been her friend and not her enemy.

'He's a dangerous man, Aliénor. He's the one who decides exactly what information the French people should have. He's the one whipping up hatred of the Jews and the gypsies, the communists and the homosexuals.' After a pause Ralf added, 'You know, *we're* kept in the dark too.' Like Aliénor, he kept his voice low. Others might hear. 'My brother's out in Russia. With Paulus's Sixth Army. At Stalingrad. We haven't had any news from him since before Christmas.'

Five months. It was confirmation of a sort of what the pamphlets the RAF dropped had said, that the Germans had suffered a heavy defeat. She should have been elated, but instead her heart was tight with compassion for the man before her. Tragedy touched both sides in a war. 'Oh, Ralf, that's awful.' She brought her fingers to his cheek. 'I'm so sorry.'

All at once she felt drained. She pulled away from him, just as the music finished. 'I must go now, Ralf. Good-night.'

4

She waited until the sounds of the house had died around her. The clock on the landing halfway down the stairs struck eleven. Another half an hour went by before she got out of bed, pulled on her long silk dressing gown and slipped out of her room. The dark wasn't a problem. She'd lived here all her life and could have walked every inch of the château blindfold. Snores came from her father's suite of rooms, from her mother's silence.

Every sense was alert as she moved down the stairs. She had her excuses ready if she were caught: 'I'm hungry, I'm going to raid the pantry' if she were inside, and 'I needed some fresh air' if she were in the château grounds. Anyone seeing her in her night clothes and barefoot would be sure to believe her. Or so she reasoned. The thought didn't slow her heartbeat. She mustn't be caught outside after curfew. The Germans were ruthless in the way they kept the population obedient and amenable. Capture would mean deportation. Or even death.

Thirty-six hours had passed, a day and a half of sick fizzing impatience and churning anxiety. She'd forced herself to keep as much as possible to her normal routine, but hadn't dared risk going to the hut while the Gestapo were still at the château.

Colonel Ostermeyer and his men had left in the afternoon, to the relief of everyone, Aliénor sensed, including the regular army officers. Snatches of overheard conversation made her think they were going south towards Poitiers, stopping on the way at Mirebeau. Until she went to the hut and saw for herself, she had no way of knowing if they'd found the saboteur, but their unsmiling faces as they piled into their cars and sped off down the drive gave her a joyous hope that they'd failed.

Once outside, she had to stop to allow her eyes to adjust. The night was cloudless, and the stars and the waning moon threw a faint unearthly gleam over grass, hedges, trees. Aliénor picked her way, crossing paths and lawns. The grass was cold and damp beneath her bare feet, and gravel dug into them. The bark of a fox, the eerie hoo-hoo of a tawny owl, the rustling and snuffling of a hedgehog — such familiar night-time noises normally — threatened to spook her tonight. She moved soundlessly past the north wing of the château where the German officers and men were billeted. Even though she knew he'd left, she pictured Colonel Ostermeyer standing at a window watching her every movement, and the hairs at the back of her neck stood on end.

Her immediate destination was thankfully close by. Tucked away behind the thick trunk of an oak tree was a stone-built structure where discarded garden furniture was kept. Here Aliénor pulled on over her pyjamas the clothes she'd stowed beneath a pile of chairs earlier in the day: a loose shirt of coarse linen, heavy-duty dark blue trousers that she gathered at the waist with a leather belt, and a long-sleeved high-necked wool jersey. She laced leather shoes on her feet. The wooden clogs the locals wore wouldn't do. She must make no sound.

Heart beating fast still, Aliénor picked up the bandages and the cloth-tied bundle of eggs, cheese and bread she'd also left there earlier, and set out.

A high stone wall ran all the way round the château grounds. At the part of it Aliénor headed for, rain and frost and ivy had eaten away at the mortar between the stones and they'd come tumbling down, leaving deep u-shaped gaps like empty sockets in a row of teeth. Aliénor clambered over the lowest of the gaps, standing stock-still when a loose stone rumbled to the ground.

Nothing. No one. With relief, she carried on. The night air was cool, and a cruel wind had picked up. She was glad she'd put the jersey on. She was following a wide path that ran between woodland on one side, and on the other, a field of some crop she couldn't make out in the feeble light from the moon and the stars. The land itself was pitch black. The farmhouses that she knew were there somewhere in the darkness were tightly shuttered, as the Germans required. A barn owl, ghostly white, glided past, and she sucked in a sharp breath, sure it was a spectre sent by the colonel, come to fetch her back. Something large blundered through the undergrowth.

It was a nightmare journey, the first time she'd had to make it at night. Every metre of the three-kilometre trek seemed fraught with danger. At last she reached her destination, the vineyard enclosed on three sides by thick woodland. It was she who had chosen the hideout, and in all modesty she knew it was a good choice. A dispute over the succession had left the vineyard abandoned, the vines and weeds growing tall and rangy. In one corner stood a small stone-built hut where grape-pickers could eat and rest. The side visible from the path was crumbling and covered by a thicket of brambles. It, too, looked abandoned.

Aliénor stood some fifty metres away, her back to a tree, and listened. Night noises — the bark of a dog, the screech of an owl — came to her through the chill air. But no shuffling of feet in the woods behind her, or smell of tobacco. No muted talk or rattle of rifles. She listened for a long time, until she was satisfied. At last she went up to the hut, cautious still, moved round to the back and rapped four regular beats on the low door.

'Christian,' she called softly.

From inside, a quiet, 'Who is it?'

'Mélisande.'

The air inside the hut was stuffy, stale. The room smelt of sweat and cold cinders from the fire. Closing the door behind her, Christian stepped to the mantelpiece. The light from a single candle barely pierced the darkness. He picked it up, tilting it to light a second candle stuck to a saucer by a pool of cooled wax.

'I've brought food,' she said, keeping her voice low still. 'And fresh bandages.' Her gaze went to the figure who lay unmoving on the bed along the far wall, a darker shadow amongst the shadows all around. 'How is he?'

Taking the candle from Christian, she crossed to the bed and knelt beside it. The Englishman lay on his back. His eyes were closed, she saw. He was asleep.

Christian came to stand beside her. 'His face and hands seem to be healing well. I've taken the bandages off his hands. That way the air can get at the skin.'

'Good.' Holding the candle high, Aliénor ran her gaze over the strong lines of the Englishman's face, the dark

arching eyebrows, the three days'
growth of beard. Christian was right,
she thought, relieved: the scabs were
dry and didn't look inflamed. 'Let's
have a look at his leg.'

She reached out, intending to push
back the blanket that covered him
— and her eyes flew wide when the
Englishman's fingers closed round her
wrist. He'd woken up. A shock of
awareness sped through her at his
touch. His hand was warm, and rough
with scabs.

'What are you doing?'

'I'm going to change the bandages on
your leg.'

His hand fell back to the bed. He
grimaced, and she knew his leg must be
giving him a great deal of pain. 'What's
the news from the outside world?' he
asked in his slightly accented French.

'Well, the Germans haven't caught
you yet.'

There was a moment's silence, and
Aliénor wondered if she'd gone too far
with this dangerous man. But he

smiled, and she drew in a shaky breath and started peeling off the first of the bandages. 'The Gestapo colonel and his men,' she went on, 'left earlier today. They're going to spend the night near Mirebeau, then going on to Poitiers in the morning.' She twisted round to look up at Christian.

He nodded. 'I'll get the message through.'

'How is it, my leg? Tell me the truth.'

'I'm not sure,' she said, trying to hide her concern. The skin around the injury was pink and rather too warm. 'Bear in mind it's going to take longer to heal than your face and hands.'

★ ★ ★

The servants, the few that the war hadn't taken away for one reason or another, were busy cooking and preparing rooms for three important visitors, Auguste and Hortense d'Eparnelle and their son Henri.

Aliénor's marriage to Henri d'Eparnelle

had been arranged some years before. It was the perfect match: a family rich as Croesus but newly arrived in society, relatively speaking, was uniting with an impoverished but aristocratic family that could trace its lineage back to before the First Crusade. The purpose of the visit was to enable the two young people most concerned to meet and get to know each other, and for the two families to agree on a date.

'Stand up straight, Aliénor,' her mother ordered. 'Hold your hands together in front of you. Look demure.'

Aliénor stood flanked by her parents at the top of the two shallow flights of steps that curved up to meet the imposing entrance doors to the Château de la Tour Dragondas. It was almost lunchtime, and the taxi from the station in nearby Loudun was due some time soon. Her hair hung in a long thick mass down her back. She wore the dress she'd worn two evenings before. If Théodore Gaillard's reaction was anything to go by, then the dress with its sprigs of vibrant pink roses printed on a white background did indeed flatter her. The thought didn't please her. She wanted only to cry.

'This is the twentieth century, *mère*,' she'd protested that morning over breakfast. She didn't know how long she'd been arguing with her mother. Her throat was raw and her head ached. They'd had the same argument many times before. 'People don't go into arranged marriages nowadays.' All at once the image of the Englishman as she'd seen him last came into her mind. She shook her head, briefly troubled.

Her mother's lips pursed. 'It's your duty, Aliénor,' she said, 'to keep our land in the family.'

Aliénor had cried out in bitter anger. It was futile. Her words had fallen, as before, on deaf ears. She'd pushed herself up from the table and run out of the room.

Remembering the episode, she felt new anger stir. Her eyes, she knew, were red-rimmed and swollen. Darkly shadowed, too, by lack of sleep the night before. Her expression was mutinous, sullen. Sickly, she wondered what impression she'd make on Henri d'Eparnelle.

Her first impression was one of relief. She watched as a shiny open-top carriage pulled by two horses came up the drive and drew to a halt in front of them. A tall heavily built man in a tweed suit that was a fraction too loose for him, and a sharp-faced woman wearing green — Henri's parents, of course, were helped down by a servant. At the same time, a man in his late forties jumped down from the rear seat of the carriage and hastened round to the other side to pull down the step for the final passenger.

Henri d'Eparnelle, tall, slim and long-legged, stepped down. He wore a dog's-tooth-check jacket, trousers that matched the deep brown check in the jacket, and two-tone brown and beige shoes. He was quite a few years older than she was, thirty-one to her eighteen, but he was good-looking and he dressed impeccably, she thought, watching as he brushed a fleck of something from the sleeve of his jacket. Maybe things wouldn't be so bad after all.

'Remember what I told you.' Thérèse whispered the warning while the d'Eparnelles were still some ten metres away. A bright smile of welcome was fixed on her face. 'If the marriage doesn't go through, we lose all this.'

The movement of her eyes encompassed the building behind her, the grounds all around, and the farms and forests, towns and villages that formed the rest of the estate. Five or ten minutes before, Aliénor's reply would probably have sounded headstrong and rebellious. But now her eyes were on Henri d'Eparnelle, hope high in her breast. 'Say little. Smile a lot. Say or do nothing controversial. Don't worry, *mère*. I'll be as good as gold.'

The d'Eparnelles climbed the entrance

steps, the two older ones slowly, Henri rather faster, and the two families greeted each other, handshakes between the men, and kisses for the women. As he stood before her, Aliénor wondered if Henri would kiss her, and didn't know whether to be upset or otherwise when he clasped her hand in his in the very briefest of handshakes.

'It's good to meet you at last, Aliénor.' His voice was strong and deeply masculine. His cologne, a subtle citrus scent, wafted around him. 'You look lovely in that dress,' he said.

'Thank you.' Aliénor smiled. From the corner of her eye, she saw both sets of parents exchange looks.

'A pleasant journey, Auguste?' asked Aliénor's father as the carriage headed back down the drive, cracking the gravel beneath its heavy iron-rimmed wheels.

'Ha! The train was crowded. And that taxi is a real bone-shaker. I'm aching all over.'

It was said with humour, and Thérèse

smiled. 'Shall we go in? I expect you'd like to see your rooms and freshen up before lunch.'

Lunch was a stilted affair at first. The setting — the small dining room whose French windows opened out on to the sun-filled terrace — was perfect; and the food — fish caught in the château lake, two roast chickens, a goat's cheese, and plums bottled the previous autumn, all washed down by several bottles of wine, the best her father could provide — was surprisingly good, considering the Germans had requisitioned so much. Henri, she noted with approval, stuck to water after an initial half glass of her father's red.

The conversation, however, came in bursts punctuated by short awkward silences. It wasn't a social event, of course, so much as a business lunch. Both sets of parents were nervous. Pausing before speaking, they picked their words with care. Aliénor's parents' anxiety, well-hidden behind gracious manners, was easy to understand: a lot of money was riding on this marriage. But she was less sure of the reasons for her future parents-in-law's tension.

Part of it, Aliénor knew, was because the d'Eparnelles didn't know the Rochefontaine de Montforts all that well. Even though the two families were to be united by marriage, neither could be wholly certain where the other's sympathies lay. Were the d'Eparnelles patriots, hoping France would one day be free again? Or were they collaborators, working with the Germans and willing to denounce their fellow citizens if the occasion arose? Aliénor kept silent for the most part, as her mother had instructed, but she could sense each family feeling their way, sounding the other out. It was a sad reflection, she thought bitterly, on what her country had become under German occupation.

Time after time, her gaze was drawn to Henri, who sat diagonally opposite her. An involuntary smile curved her mouth. With his strong-boned face and dark blue eyes, he was an attractive man.

'The plan is, when Henri moves down here, all being well . . . ' Auguste d'Eparnelle picked up his chicken leg and bit into it with gusto. 'Go on, you tell them, son.'

Aliénor found she liked Henri's father. A straightforward man of undoubted charm, he had a hearty appetite and a clear enjoyment of life.

'If this war ever ends, we're going to build a factory nearby, as arranged.' Henri spoke decisively, a man who knew what he was doing. 'But we're also going to build a village of five hundred houses for the workers. Quality houses with indoor plumbing and gardens so people can grow their own vegetables.'

Vincent Rochefontaine de Montfort's eyebrows shot up. 'A village, you say? More like a town.'

'You're so right, Vincent!' Henri's mother tinkled a laugh.

'I think it's marvellous,' said Aliénor.

'All those houses.' She dropped her gaze, cheeks burning, when everyone, and especially Henri, turned to look at her.

As he had done the evening before with Colonel Ostermeyer and Théodore Gaillard, Aliénor's father took Auguste d'Eparnelle on a tour of the interior of the château after lunch, while Henri said he was going to explore the grounds. The maid brought ersatz coffee and a dish of dainty cakes into the dining room for the ladies.

Henri's mother wrinkled her nose at the coffee. She sat forward, her face close to Thérèse's, and lowered her voice. 'I must say, the young things seem to have hit it off very well.' Aliénor bristled. Hortense d'Eparnelle appeared to have forgotten she was there.

'They do, don't they?' Thérèse looked relieved that the first hurdle had been cleared. 'A *petit four*, Hortense?' she asked, holding out the dish.

'Thank you.' She took one and bit

into it. 'Tell me, Thérèse, does your daughter have problems with hay fever? Her eyes are very red.'

Aliénor bunched her hands together on her lap, too busy with her thoughts to hear Thérèse's reply. The two women would be examining her teeth next.

Hortense leaned even closer to Thérèse and dropped her voice to a whisper. 'Henri has kept himself pure for his bride, you know. I insisted on it.'

For the space of a second, there was silence. It was an extraordinary pronouncement. Aliénor sat up in her chair, annoyance giving way to incredulity. All at once she wanted to laugh. How on earth could his mother know? Though hazy on the detail, Aliénor knew this was something people usually did in the privacy of their room. So how true could the claim be? If it were true, it showed almost saintly restraint in a virile young man.

Thérèse, plainly as astonished as her daughter by Hortense's words, seemed to collect herself. 'That's good to hear,' she said. 'As has Aliénor, of course, for her future husband. That goes without saying.' She turned sharp eyes on her daughter. 'Go and find Henri, Aliénor. Talk to him. Get to know him a little better.'

As she left the dining room, she heard Hortense say, 'Well, she's tall and has got good bones.' Aliénor gritted her teeth. Good child-bearing hips too? she wondered. Obedient to her mother, however, she kept the thought to herself.

5

She found Henri down by the lake, standing beside the man she'd assumed was his servant who sat on a fold-up chair in front of an easel, a piece of charcoal in his hand.

'Olivier Papineau,' Henri said by way of introduction.

'*Mademoiselle*.' Clever eyes, a ready smile and a bow of the head greeted her. The office worker's uniform of suit, shirt and tie that he wore looked out of place in this peaceful pastoral setting.

'My personal assistant,' Henri added.

'An artist too, I see,' Aliénor said, looking at the easel.

From where they stood, the main part and most of the south wing of the château were visible. Its high arched windows and vast slate roofs glimmered in the sunlight. All of this had been captured in exquisite detail on the page of the sketchpad open on the easel. Aliénor watched with Henri as Olivier shaded in a group of trees that stood on a low rise to the north of the château.

'That was where the original tower stood,' she said. 'Dragondas was one of the lords who fought with Charles Martel against the Saracens in the battle of Poitiers in 732. He was given these lands — ' She gestured around her. ' — in recompense. He built the tower and called it Montfort.'

As if by some tacit agreement, she and Henri moved off in the direction of the château, leaving Olivier by the lake.

'The main building,' she went on, 'dates from the end of the twelfth century. A Montfort ancestor fought beside Guy de Lusignan in the Holy Land — '

' — and as a reward he was given more land and the money to put up a suitably lavish building.'

Aliénor laughed. 'Well I wouldn't go that far. The original building was just a big hall with a few rooms attached, but you get the drift.' They walked side by side, an unhurried, companionable stroll. The shouts and occasional revving of an engine from the north wing seemed very far away. 'The two wings were added in the early eighteen hundreds, and the main part was completely rebuilt then. Napoleon's thank-you for loyal service,' she said with a smiling glance at Henri. 'Vespasien Rochefontaine de Montfort was at his side all the way to Russia and back.'

'Clearly a born survivor. Russia, and before that the Revolution.'

Aliénor laughed again. 'He spent those years in America. We Rochefontaine de Montforts are a clever lot, you see. We've managed to be on the winning side at most of the great moments of history.'

She'd meant it as a light-hearted remark. But Henri stopped, turning to face her. His expression was serious. 'And profited each time, it would appear. So, what about now?' They were about fifty metres from the château, and the shouts, barked orders and crunch of many boots across gravel were louder, more intrusive now. 'Do you think you're on the winning side this time?'

Aliénor flushed at the implied criticism, but the softly voiced question made her wary. She kept her tone neutral. 'We didn't invite the Germans here. They commandeered the château. We had no choice.'

Her thoughts went back to the drinks party — one of many — two evenings before, and she recalled with a certain shame the extent of the hospitality her parents extended to the German officers. But she remembered too the day in June 1940 when the Germans entered the nearby town of Loudun and paraded their victory in front of the town hall. She and her cousin Joséphine had been there with her father watching the lines of soldiers march past. His mouth had crumpled in that stiff way of a man determined not to cry. A single tear had slid down his cheek and he turned away, turning her and Joséphine with him, unable to watch any more, the words 'A black day for France' almost choking in his throat. Yes, she knew which side her father had chosen. Whether it was the side that would win was another matter.

'We're lodging them,' she said. 'Your firm is producing the ball bearings they need for their war effort. Is there really any difference?'

'You're right, of course. But don't forget the Germans would have closed the factories down if we hadn't cooperated.' He was speaking about the two factories near Saint Velérien that were the source of the family's wealth. There was bitterness in his voice. 'Or confiscated them.' He glanced towards the lake, then back at her, and he smiled, a seemingly genuine smile. He nodded towards the château. 'It looks like your father has finished giving mine the grand tour. Let's join them.'

Both sets of parents had come out on

to the terrace. A maid brought a bottle of white wine, glasses and a packet of cigarettes on a tray which she put down on one of the low tables.

'A glass of wine for you?' Henri asked as they ran up the steps which led to the terrace. She shook her head and watched as he went over to the others. Auguste looked at his son, glanced across at Aliénor where she stood at the top of the steps, and looked again at Henri, who nodded. It was a pantomime of unvoiced communication that had lasted a bare two seconds, but that nod of Henri's appeared to indicate she had passed the test.

While the others settled into the armchairs, Aliénor turned and leant her elbows on the balustrade, crumbling and powdery in places, which edged the terrace. In the distance a hen harrier circled slow and low over the wild beauty of the grounds. Olivier was still at his easel by the lake. The afternoon was mild and still, a perfect May day.

Her parents would be pleased, at

least. But she wasn't sure what *she* felt about the prospect of marriage to Henri d'Eparnelle. She wasn't so naïve as to expect tender words of undying love from her suitor. So what had she expected? Some warmth, perhaps? He came across as a cold man, a man very much in control of his emotions. And, except to shake her hand, he hadn't touched her once. Unbidden, the memory slipped into her mind of the Englishman's warm, strong fingers sliding down her arm, and she shivered.

When Henri joined her, swirling the wine in his glass, she forced herself to hide her misgivings. 'No cigarette?' she said with a smile.

'No.' He didn't smile back. 'Disgusting habit.' His sweeping gesture took in the lawns, the lake beyond, and the thick woodland on the horizon. 'It's a beautiful place.'

Aliénor lifted her elbows from the balustrade. Crumbs of the soft local stone were sticking to her forearms. 'Are you really sure you want to take it on?' she asked, brushing them off.

His eyes met hers. She held her breath, aware of the unspoken question behind the one she'd asked.

'Of course,' he said, and turned away.

★ ★ ★

The next morning she was relieved that Henri seemed to sense she wanted time to herself. She sat on a rug by the lakeside, pulling her knees up to her chin and clasping her hands round them. A short while before, Henri had walked with her and Olivier to the lake, had spread the rug for her, and now stood a few metres away, watching his assistant sketch the pigeon tower on the far side and the woodland beyond. She could hear the murmur of their voices from behind her and the occasional burst of laughter from Vincent and Auguste, who were fishing further along, while Thérèse and Hortense walked down to the church in the village.

A light wind rippled the water, swaying the tall reeds on her left. Damsel flies, a brilliant iridescent blue in the sunlight, hovered centimetres above the surface before darting away. Aliénor wished her thoughts could be as smooth and untroubled as the scene in front of her.

The man she was due to marry was presentable and likeable. She knew her heart wasn't engaged, but then neither was his. He was pleasantly indifferent to her, in fact. She sighed. Perhaps love would grow on both sides.

If only she had someone she could talk to about it. Her best friend and confidante, her cousin Joséphine, had died the year before of scarlet fever. And she couldn't look to her mother for answers. Their relationship was too distant for that. Besides, Thérèse — and her father, of course — desperately wanted this marriage. It would bring much-needed money into the family.

Despite her misgivings, Aliénor knew

she had little choice but to agree to the marriage. Or rather, to make no objection. To her intense annoyance, both sets of parents had already taken her agreement for granted. The ceremony would take place the day before Christmas the following year, she was informed. 'Perhaps the war will be over by then,' Auguste said.

Mid-afternoon on the Sunday, the taxi arrived and the d'Eparnelles took their leave. The goodbyes were amicable. Aliénor could tell her parents considered it had been a successful weekend. She found she was holding her breath as Henri came up to her to say goodbye. She caught the citrus tang of his cologne as he bent towards her. It was a delicate kiss, a light brushing of his lips on hers that set her heartbeat racing. The first of many kisses from the man she would marry, she thought, watching as the carriage took him away down the drive.

* * *

Aliénor felt sick. She exchanged a bleak look with Christian, who squatted beside her by the bed in the grape-pickers' hut. The shutter of the hut's only window was partly open, and a rectangle of sunlight spilled on to the Englishman's leg.

It was Monday afternoon. Henri and his parents had left the day before. She wished she'd been able to get up to the hut in the morning. Not that it would have made much difference, she thought with dismay.

She pushed the last of the yarrow and bandages aside and looked again at the long jagged injury that ran from ankle to knee. Most of it was healing well. The yarrow had done its work — a minor miracle, surely, given the unhygienic conditions she'd had to work in. The edges had stayed together, and were dry and scabbing nicely. The part nearest the knee, however, was red and swollen and oozing pus. Aliénor touched the skin close to where the wound was still raw and open, and the

Englishman flinched, his mouth twisting into a grimace.

'It's started to throb,' he said. There was silence: all three of them knew what that meant. 'But no doctors,' he went on. His voice was a growl, his expression grim. 'I'd be putting the two of you and the whole of the local network in danger. I can't risk it.' His face had lost its deathly pallor, and five days' growth of beard softened its strong lines. But Aliénor saw how often he winced and jounced his leg, and knew he was in greater pain than he let on.

A fly buzzed angrily and settled on the raw flesh. Aliénor flicked it away with a cry of disgust. Her eyes met the Englishman's. 'We might not have the choice, Weyland,' she warned, stumbling over the pronunciation.

'Peter. My name's Peter,' he growled.

'So what do we do?' Christian pushed himself upright, his voice taut with worry.

Aliénor too stood up. 'I think I

should go down to the village and see Aunt Apolline.'

She looked to Christian for confirmation. He nodded, eyes narrowing behind the thick lenses of his glasses. 'The wise woman. Yes.'

'I've got my bicycle.'

She'd come to the hut by a long, circuitous route, at times pushing her bike along the hidden paths through the woods, using the jungle of ferns and spiky broom, almost as tall as she was, as cover, the need for caution dictating her actions. The Gestapo had left, but the soldiers stationed at the château were still making regular patrols and searches.

Aliénor was out of breath when she reached Apolline's house at the end of a narrow lane that led off the main road through the village. Propping her bicycle against the wall, she knocked on the door.

'I hope I'm not interrupting you,' she said, kissing Apolline on her cheeks, dry and thin as paper. The smell of something savoury was thick in the air, making her mouth water, and for a second or two she forgot her worries about the Englishman.

'No, my dear *mademoiselle* Aliénor. You're welcome at any time.' In her seventies, she wore a long-sleeved blouse and an ankle-length skirt, both rusty black and reminiscent of the turn of the century, protected by a dark wraparound apron. Her iron-grey hair was drawn into a loose bun at her nape in a style that had been popular when she was a young woman. 'Come on in. Sit yourself down. You'll have some soup, won't you?'

'Thank you. Just a little.' Apolline would be offended if she refused her hospitality. Food was in short supply, though, and precious, and she mustn't take too much. She crossed to the table that stood by the window of the large sparsely furnished room, aware that the old woman's shrewd eyes were following her. Bunches of herbs hung from nails in the beams, black with age, which spanned the ceiling. Some were for flavouring food, while others were for medicinal use. Various home-made remedies were stored in the jars that covered the mantelpiece.

'I want to thank you for delivering Suzanne's baby,' Aliénor said, sitting down. Keeping to her normal routine as much as possible while the Gestapo were at the château, she'd called in on Suzanne and had been delighted to find that mother and child, and young Jérôme, were all doing well.

'A fine baby girl.' Apolline moved briskly, lifting a steaming cast-iron pot off the hook above the logs in the fireplace and putting it on the table, followed by two shallow china dishes, their glazing crazed with age. 'An easy birth, thank goodness. Life's difficult enough for her as it is,' she added with a sigh, ladling soup into one of the dishes and pushing it across the table.

'Yes,' Aliénor agreed quietly. The birth of a healthy baby was a time for joy. But Suzanne's husband had been a prisoner of war in Germany for the best part of three years. Aliénor couldn't help wondering how he'd react when he returned home, as he surely would one day, to find he was a father again after his long absence.

'Well, you're not unwell, I'd say.' Apolline sat down opposite her. Holding a half-loaf of bread to her chest, she cut off a slice and passed it across the table. 'Although you look as if you've been under a great deal of strain lately.' Her tone was kind, and she paused for a second, inviting Aliénor to explain if she wanted to. 'So what can I do for you?'

Aliénor was conscious of the blood pounding in her ears. The moment had come. Instinctively she knew she could trust the wise woman. She wouldn't have come here otherwise. But there was always the possibility, lurking like a hidden cancer at the back of her mind, that the old woman would listen, then rush to denounce her to the authorities.

She ran her tongue round her dry

mouth. 'Someone I know has hurt his leg. I think it's infected. It looks and feels all spongy. It's very tender.' She broke off as a log shifted in the fireplace, making her jump, fraying ragged nerves still further.

Apolline sat back in her chair, her gaze never leaving Aliénor's face. 'You haven't told me how this person hurt his leg, but if it's showing signs of infection now, whatever it was must have happened a few days ago.' Her tone was speculative, and again she paused, as if prompting the young woman opposite her to fill the silence. 'Last Thursday or Friday, perhaps.' She wetted her bread in the soup and bit off a mouthful, chewing it slowly. 'Thursday was a busy day for the Germans here in the village. Well, you were here. You saw them.'

Aliénor nodded, forcing herself to meet the old woman's scrutiny. Apolline was bound to be curious, but her conjectures were uncomfortably close to the mark.

'Louis tells me they were looking for someone they call the Smith.' Her nephew Louis taught German in the *lycée* in Loudun. 'I would hazard a guess they haven't found him yet.' She swallowed another mouthful of bread and added, 'Have they, my dear?'

The implication was obvious. Colour rushed into Aliénor's cheeks. She looked down at the table, picked up her spoon and raised a spoonful of soup to her mouth. But her hand wasn't quite steady and some of it spilled back into the dish.

She put the spoon down and looked at the wise woman. 'How would I know? I don't know anything about any of that,' she said, keeping her tone carefully neutral.

Apolline held her gaze before nodding, a smile hovering over her lips. She pulled back the net curtain and looked out of the window. Two ewes, each with an almost full-grown lamb, grazed, out of sight, if not out of earshot of the Germans, behind the high stone walls of Apolline's courtyard.

The old woman let the curtain drop and stood up. 'Wait here. Finish your soup. I've got what you need.'

Aliénor too got to her feet. 'Can I help?'

'No. Best not. Sit down and finish your soup,' Apolline said, going to the door that led out to the courtyard.

She came back some fifteen minutes later, holding a small linen bag held closed by a drawstring.

'We'll try this,' she said, 'but if the infection is no better in two days, bring him here and I'll get a doctor to come. I know which ones I can trust.'

Aliénor shuddered with the first stirrings of revulsion as she took the bag. She had a fair idea of what it contained. Was it her imagination, or could she feel a fine movement as she held it on her outstretched palm?

Aunt Apolline reached out to Aliénor's hand and pulled the drawstring open. 'See this?' she said. 'This inner bag? Spread it over the injury and hold it in place with a bandage.'

Aliénor looked down at the bag in her hand. Inside, she could see black lace, cut from a mourning veil perhaps, that had been washed so often it was now a dirty grey. Behind the coarse mesh, tiny creamy-white creatures moved, and she shuddered again in the age-old reaction to what she saw.

'Don't let them out of that inner bag whatever you do,' the old woman was saying, 'otherwise they'll get everywhere.'

Maggots. They would eat the rotten flesh and spare the good. Aliénor swallowed hard and lifted troubled eyes to the wise woman.

'Let's hope I'm in time,' she said in a voice that shook.

6

'Jesus,' the Englishman growled. 'I'm back in the Middle Ages. It'll be leeches next.'

Kneeling beside the makeshift bed in the grape-pickers' hut, Aliénor heard the grim humour, but she also saw the grimace that twisted his lips and the look of distaste that crossed his features as she took the lace pouch out of its drawstring bag. Late-afternoon sunlight came in through the partly open door and the high window next to it, chasing the shadows away. She held the pouch gingerly, dangling between thumb and index finger. It shivered with movement, and her stomach turned, sickness rising. Countless tiny creatures, each no bigger than half a grain of rice, moved busily behind the coarse mesh of the lace.

'It does seem rather primitive,' she

murmured. Cobbled together by Aunt Apolline out of old discoloured lace, the pouch was designed to stop the creatures straying. At the same time, they could poke their mouth-hooks through the mesh and do their cleansing, healing work. She shuddered, revulsion at the method tangling with pity for the man she was about to inflict it on.

Christian, standing behind her, shifted uncomfortably. 'I've heard this sort of thing saved a lot of lives in the first war.'

'By accident,' the Englishman cut in. 'The maggots had got in before the soldiers could be brought to hospital.'

'We've got to do it,' Aliénor said as a fresh wave of sickness rose. 'We don't have any alternative.'

'Agreed.' The Englishman closed his eyes, as if the exchange, or the infection in his leg, had sapped his strength, and flopped back against the wall of the hut that served as a headboard to his bed, sending a cloud of fine mud and stone dust into the air. Sweat stood out on his forehead, and darkened and curled his hair. 'It hurts like hell,' he said, 'and the throbbing is worse.'

Aliénor forced herself to look at the leg wound. He was right: it had become worse in the two hours it had taken her to go down to the wise woman's and back. The skin around it was an angry red, puffy and too dry, while the raw flesh, an angry red too, was moist and streaked with whitish-yellow pus. There was a sickly hint of sweetness in the air around it. Aliénor gulped, once, twice, to keep the nausea down.

'What can I do?' asked Christian.

She turned to look up at him. He'd taken his glasses off and was rubbing his eyes, dark-shadowed like the Englishman's.

'You look tired,' she said. 'Why don't you try and get some sleep? I can stay here a little while longer.' She turned back to the Englishman, aware that he watched, his face taut with pain as she smoothed the pouch over the infection, making sure every part of the wound was covered.

'I was up most of the night,' Christian said. 'I needed to find out if the other two got back safely.' Which meant that he'd cycled, as he'd done many times before, some thirty kilometres, in defiance of the curfew, using back lanes and tracks, to meet his contact in Scévolles forest. Sixty kilometres in one night, the fear of being caught by the Germans a constant harrowing presence. Aliénor was filled with admiration for this earnest, studious, unassuming man. 'They did,' he added, handing her several strips of linen before heading for the door. 'I'll be nearby. There's a place in the vines that's hidden. I'll get some sleep there, while the sun lasts.'

Aliénor watched as he ducked his head under the lintel and went outside. Taking the longest bandage, she wrapped it round and round the Englishman's leg, keeping the pouch and its squirming contents securely in place.

'There,' she said, tying the ends of the bandage in a knot, relieved the ordeal was over at last. About to get to her feet, she made a sound of surprise when his hand curled round her wrist, staying her. Once again she felt the touch of his fingers. Her gaze flew to his face.

'I'm grateful for all you've done,' he said. 'Thank you.' There was a bleakness in his smile that made her heart go out to him, and she could make no protest when he brought her hand up in such a way that her fingertips brushed across his beard-rough cheek. He pressed a kiss to the inside of her wrist, his lips warm and dry on her skin.

The gesture was so shockingly intimate that for long seconds she was unable to speak. 'You must pull through,' she said at last. Her voice was husky.

'I fully intend to.' But he flinched as he spoke, and jerked his knee up towards his body.

'Can you feel them?' Aliénor closed

her eyes for an instant. It didn't bear thinking about.

'A little. Like creepy-crawlies tickling me.'

She had to work to keep the tears back. 'Go to sleep. I'll watch over you,' she said, and felt she was losing part of herself as his hand slid from her arm.

★   ★   ★

Aliénor felt a spurt of alarm as she stepped outside the hut. It was late. She'd stayed watching over the Englishman far longer than she'd intended. The sun had disappeared behind the black clouds piling up in the southwest, darkening an already sombre sky with the threat of rain.

There was a chill in the air, and she shivered as she watched Christian thread his way between the vines, heading towards her. Her mother would be furious. She gave her daughter a great deal of freedom, knowing that the people on the vast Rochefontaine de Montfort estate or the Germans at the château would never harm her. Even so, Aliénor was expected to be home for the evening meal at the latest.

'I'll come with you,' Christian said as he drew nearer.

She shook her head. 'No. It might be dangerous for you.'

She kissed him goodbye, then swung her bicycle round, jumped on and started pedalling fast back down the lane. Though it was several hours before the curfew, it wasn't a good idea to be out in the gathering dusk.

She slowed down only when she came to the village that lay two kilometres from the château. The pale façades of houses and shops looked dull in the growing darkness. Most of the shopkeepers and householders had already pulled their shutters closed for fear the British and American bombers would target their property.

As she passed it, the door of the café opened. Yellow light and a burst of laughter spilled out. The man coming out of the café waved at her, called a slurred 'Goodnight, *mademoiselle*,' and set off in the direction she had come from.

'Goodnight, *monsieur* Raymond,' she called after him. 'Take care.'

It was some twenty metres further on as she came level with the forge that she ran into the patrol. A German soldier stepped out of the shadows, his hand raised. His helmet gleamed dully in the feeble light.

'Stop. Get down off your bicycle. Show me your papers.'

His French was poor but understand-able, and Aliénor got off her bicycle. Holding it up by the handlebars, she took her identity card from the pocket of her skirt and handed it to him. He was possibly one of the soldiers billeted at the château, but she didn't recognise him. The insignia on his sleeve made her think he was a sergeant.

He glanced at her, opened her identity card, and shining a torch on it, began to read. The features of her face must be hard to make out in the deepening gloom, Aliénor thought. The man was wasting his time. This wasn't the first time she had been stopped. The trick was not to do or say anything to antagonise them. So she stood, immobile, and said nothing. A second soldier had stayed in the shadows, she saw. Back-up if there was trouble. From the forge on her right came men's voices and the hammering of metal on metal. A dog barked in a distant house, and fell silent.

The sergeant snapped the card shut and looked over at her. 'Little Miss Moneybags, eh?' His lips curled in contempt.

Aliénor shook her head, unsure what to do. His assertion was so far from the truth as to be laughable. 'No,' she said cautiously.

The flat of his palm slammed into her ear and she recoiled in shock, staggering back, fighting to keep her balance.

'Don't argue.' And to the other man, 'Search her.'

It all happened so fast. The first soldier took her bicycle from her. The second, a private, came out of the shadows, pulled her arms up and started roughly patting her down. Sweat prickled at her armpits. This had never happened before. All at once she was very frightened. It was almost dark and there was no one about. No one to help her. If only the voices inside the forge would stop and the people would come out, she thought.

She bit her lip, willing herself not to say or do anything as the private's hands lingered over her breasts, pressing and smoothing them through her jersey and camisole top. Her cheeks burned with shame. She had never been so powerless. The sergeant had pointed his torch at her and was watching. She sensed rather than saw the smile on his face, his enjoyment of her fear. The ear he'd hit pounded with an insistent, throbbing ache.

The private's hands moved down past her waist. Bending at the knees, he lifted the hem of her skirt. She made a small involuntary movement of protest and heard him give a grunt of satisfaction. He looked up at her and she saw the bright gleam in his eye, the sardonic smile on his lips. At all costs, she told herself, she mustn't react. It was what they wanted, and if thwarted they might hit her again. Or shoot her. All she could do was stand there and endure. Anger, slow and intense, mounted inside her.

With the back of one hand he knocked her legs further apart. Her skin crawled with revulsion as both hands slid up her left thigh, stroking the soft skin. Tears filled her eyes. She was in an agony of shame.

The door of the forge opened and closed, briefly lighting the scene. With a muttered oath, the private pulled himself back upright and turned to look at the rapidly approaching figure. Both soldiers snapped smartly to attention.

Aliénor's heart gave a start, like a bird that knows it will soon be free: it was Ralf.

But Captain Horelbeck's face was hard, his expression closed, and he barely looked at her. He gave an order in German and the private left, coming back moments later at the wheel of a jeep. Aliénor got into the front passenger seat, Ralf taking the place of the private at the wheel. The bicycle and the two soldiers went in the back.

The journey to the château along the narrow tree-lined roads passed in a total silence, broken only by the roar of the engine. Ralf, she sensed, was incandescent with rage, though whether his fury was directed at her or at the soldiers, or all three of them, she didn't know. She, on the other hand, was wretched beyond belief, sick with humiliation and shame. Her ear ached still.

Ralf pulled up in front of the main doors, and the two of them got out. The private took his place behind the wheel again and drove off round the back of the château.

'Come on.' Ralf ran up the steps in front of her. There was no mistaking the anger in his voice and in his actions. 'They'll put your bike away for you.' At the top, he pushed open the left-hand door.

Thérèse was crossing the hall. Two of her cousins from Le Mans were visiting, and she was dressed for the evening in a shimmering satin gown of deep purple. General Hartmann and three or four other high-ranking Germans had been invited. She looked across, eyebrows arching as her daughter and the captain came through the door. Her lips pursed. 'Good evening, Captain Horelbeck.'

'I've brought Aliénor back.'

'So I see.' Her gaze swept over her daughter's face. 'Where from, may I ask?' Her tone was carefully neutral but Aliénor knew her mother had noted her flushed cheeks and shame-filled eyes.

'From the village. It was getting

dark.' Ralf's reply was clipped. He clicked his heels together, bowed, and with a cold glance at Aliénor, he left.

Thérèse's eyes fell again on her daughter. Look and tone of voice were like ice. 'You will tell me all about it, Aliénor. Tomorrow. Immediately after breakfast.'

Aliénor could only watch in silence as her mother, with a swish of satin, disappeared through double doors into the large dining room they used for grand dinner parties. The gnawing apprehension her mother's words had brought on only compounded her burning sense of shame.

★ ★ ★

There was a chill in the air the next morning when Aliénor set out, but the risen sun gave an illusion of warmth. She wore a thick wool jersey and heavy-duty cotton trousers. Though there was nothing furtive in her movements, she didn't particularly want to advertise her excursion either, and kept close to trees and hedges. She knew exactly where she was going, and would be back in plenty of time for the after-breakfast inquisition by her mother. As she moved swiftly down past the lake and into the woods, the early-morning sounds from the north wing of the château — shouted orders and lorry doors slamming — gradually grew more distant.

She followed the woodland path, uneven and criss-crossed by the roots of trees, for more than a kilometre. At a certain point she left it, moving into the thicket of trees and bushes, taking a path narrower than a man and known only to the animals of the forest or perhaps the occasional poacher. Uprooted clumps of grass and other foliage showed boar had passed this way recently.

She came to the clearing, and a gasp of wonder lodged in her throat. She'd rarely seen it look more beautiful. Sunlight slanted down through the trees, spilling in soft patches on the woodland floor. Asphodel grew in profusion, a mass of tiny white flowers forming a bright flame of colour at the end of each tall slender stem. There was a hushed stillness in the air, as if birds and animals waited to see what she'd do next.

Aliénor breathed deeply of the fresh, clean air and smiled a smile of pure delight as the tension eased from her neck and shoulders. Stooping to pick one of the stems of asphodel, she continued on her way. She was almost there.

Her night's sleep had been troubled, and interspersed by many periods of wakefulness. But it wasn't the thought of the forthcoming dressing-down by her mother that had kept her awake. Aliénor knew she could look her mother directly in the eyes and say with all honesty that nothing had happened between her and Captain Ralf Horelbeck. And nothing ever would. Even though she frequently railed against it, she knew where her duty lay. She was also aware that she couldn't tell her mother about the encounter with the two German soldiers. Her shame, her powerlessness, were like a raw wound. She couldn't bear for it to be prodded by another. If she wanted healing, she would only find it at the spring.

The thorns of a bramble snagged at her jersey. Aliénor pulled it free and took another step forward. She had arrived.

It was a hidden, secret place. Bars of sunlight filtered down between the low, twisted branches of trees, black with age, that formed a protective semi-circle round a tumble of dark rocks. On their other side, a broad expanse of deep green ivy fell to the ground like a curtain. Aliénor approached the rocks and knelt with the sense of awe she always experienced when she came here. Reaching forward, with the tips of her fingers she touched the slow, fat bubbles that welled up out of the stone in a constant, almost noiseless flow.

It was a magical place, a place of healing. This was where she'd come when Joséphine, her cousin and best friend, had died, and when her country had capitulated to Hitler, and when German soldiers had taken over her home. This was where she needed to be today.

She laid the stem of asphodel on the rock just above the spring, a bright offering to the ancient gods of the place. Making a cup of her upturned palms, she scooped some of the water up. It was clear and cold and pure. Moving back, she sat, long legs crossed in front of her, on the woodland floor. She closed her eyes with a sigh and absorbed the almost imperceptible murmur of the water, the birdsong which slowly started up again, the rustle as a small mammal skittered through the leaves. And slowly, the soothing sounds seeped into her very being, easing away the last of the tension, as the spring cast its healing spell over her troubled spirit.

7

'The two of them have been transferred,' Ralf told her later the same day. Still smarting from the interview with her mother after breakfast, Aliénor had been crossing the terrace when the German captain intercepted her. 'They were new here — and overzealous. We will talk no more about it.'

Aliénor nodded. She was grateful to him. 'Any news of your brother?' she asked quietly.

'No,' he said, and she saw great sadness in his expression in the instant before he moved away.

The tide was turning for the Germans, Aliénor thought as she watched him head towards the north wing. It seemed likely they'd suffered a massive defeat earlier in the year in Russia.

In France too the tide was turning,

she sensed. The endless requisitions meant that food — and almost everything else — was scarce. The times were getting harder, especially for women. With so many men prisoners of war or sent to work in Germany, there was always work, but it was often poorly paid, and wages couldn't keep up with the rises in prices.

An earlier scheme offering the exchange of one prisoner of war for every three people who volunteered to work in a factory in Germany had been scrapped. In February the Germans had introduced a new law requiring all young men between the ages of twenty and twenty-two to take part in the work programme. It had become compulsory.

Her thoughts went to Christian. Only a few months earlier, he'd been training to be a teacher, the first one in his family to go on to further education. But like so many others, as a result of the new law, he'd run away to swell the ranks of the Resistance.

How many others, she wondered bitterly, had had their dreams and ambitions trampled on by the Nazis?

★ ★ ★

'*I'll* do it,' the Englishman said. He was sitting up on the bed. He must have shaved that morning, for his beard had gone, and so had his pallor. 'These things itch like blazes. Let's hope this is an end of it.'

Aliénor hoped so too. She sent a silent prayer heavenward and watched as he took Christian's penknife from him, sliced through one thickness of the linen strip close to the knot she'd tied forty-eight hours before, and started unravelling the bandage round his leg.

The afternoon sun beat down on the slate roof. Flies buzzed and squabbled. A light breeze came in through the small window and the half-opened door. It helped dissipate the heat, but not much. Aliénor eased the collar of her blouse from the back of her neck.

He pulled the last of the bandage off and Aliénor gasped, revulsion swirling inside her. The lace pouch was much fuller now, each writhing creature fat and vigorous. They had been white, now they were a pinky brown. As Aliénor realised why, nausea rose and she slammed her hand across her mouth. 'Oh!' She twisted her head away.

'Get rid of these, will you, please, Christian. Bury them in the woods somewhere.'

He spoke in an undertone, out of concern for her, she thought, and heard Christian's footsteps as he headed out of the grape-pickers' hut.

'Mélisande, my dear, it's okay.'

Her gaze met his, questioning his, before her pulses leapt and she crouched to look at the wound to his leg. The area it had covered had grown a little, but the skin around it had lost its tender puffiness, the raw flesh was a clear pink, and the sickly sweet smell had gone. There were still several weeks of healing to be got through, she thought, but the infection was no longer there and the injury was clean and healthy-looking.

She straightened, smiling a smile of pure joy. All at once he was scrambling to his feet, staggering and wincing as his injured leg touched the earth floor. He cupped her face between his hands. His face too was lit by a beaming smile, but his eyes glittered, mirrors of her own, no doubt, as his gaze held hers. He wrapped her in his arms, crushing her to his chest, and buried his face in her hair. His hands were flat against her shoulder-blades as he rocked her from side to side.

'It worked. Your miracle cure worked.' His voice was muffled but she could hear gruffness in it. She hugged him to her. She wanted to say something, but it was impossible to speak. Happiness shouldn't hurt so much, she thought. It was ridiculous to be crying when she was so happy for him.

She watched him. He stood barely a metre away, sunlight glinting off the film of soap he'd spread over his lower face and neck. Eyes narrowed in concentration, he stared at his reflection in the mirror he'd hung by a nail on the outside wall, and drew his cut-throat razor in long upward strokes along the line of his jaw and up over his cheeks. He'd washed his hair with the soap and combed it, still wet, back from his forehead. As it dried, it stood up in places in unruly spikes that she longed to smooth down again.

She watched the assured movement of the hand that held the razor. Strong hands, with long fine fingers. But he'd lost some weight, she thought, seeing the slight hollowing beneath his cheek-bones.

It was the next day. When Aliénor arrived at the grape-pickers' hut that morning, it was to learn that Christian had ridden his bicycle to Scévolles forest during the night and had returned in the early hours with the Englishman's suitcase.

'Goodness only knows how they got it from Poitiers to the forest,' Christian had said, yawning. 'Train, I suppose, and bike.'

He was sleeping now in the hut, while she stood in the doorway, leaning against the architrave. She watched the Englishman, Peter, a smile curving the corners of her mouth. Over her arm were the clean trousers and shirt he'd change into when he'd finished shaving. She traced her fingers over the well-worn cotton of the shirt.

'You look happy.' Putting the razor down, he dipped his hands in the pail on the bench in front of him and splashed water on his face. It ran in a sparkling stream down over his skin.

'I am.' Her smile deepened. 'It's lovely to see you up and about, in the fresh air, in the sun.'

She spoke the simple truth. But she was conscious at the same time of the faint unease that stirred deep inside. For she knew, even then, that there was rather more to it than that.

★　★　★

She feared for him.

'Tell me about your codename. Weyland,' she said a day or two later. They were walking side by side along a track in the woods near the hut. Spots of sunlight filtered through the branches of the trees, falling in circles of constant movement on his face. He looked a much healthier colour, the shadows beneath his eyes had gone, the infection had not come back and his leg was healing well.

'It's an old legend,' he said, and she stilled for the space of a heartbeat as he put his arm round her, pulling her to him. He would touch her, she'd discovered, with an easy familiarity that was completely alien to how things were done in her family. 'Weyland the Smith.'

She came to an abrupt halt, his arm falling from her shoulders as she turned to him. 'Weyland the Smith?' She looked at him, appalled. She had to warn him. Apolline had spoken about 'the Smith', passing on the information her nephew the schoolteacher had heard. 'They're looking for you. Not just the regular army. The Gestapo are looking for you too.'

He placed his hands on her upper arms. 'They've been looking for me, my sweet Mélisande, for the best part of six months. They haven't caught me yet.' He pulled her to him, wrapped his arms around her, his hands stroking her hair, soothing her fears, and for a while at least she was able to forget them.

Another time. They sat outside the hut on the bench along the wall that wasn't visible from the path. Only the birds in the vines and in the woods beyond could see them. 'Have you got a convincing cover story?' she asked. 'The proper documents?'

'Here. Take a look. See for yourself.'

Twisting to one side, he pulled a thin leather wallet from the back pocket of his trousers and handed it to her.

'It's a forgery, I take it,' she said, unfolding the wallet and scanning the identity card inside, looking for discrepancies, mistakes. 'Was it you who chose the name Laval?' There was amused disbelief in her voice.

'You don't like my choice?' There was amusement in his voice too.

She tilted her head to look round at him. Their eyes met and held, and their faces relaxed into smiles. It was a moment to be savoured, a moment of complicity, of shared appreciation of the irony, for the Englishman had taken the surname of Pierre Laval, the arch-collaborator of the Vichy government.

Her smile lingered as she looked again at his identity card. She had no doubt it had been produced by an expert, but for her own peace of mind, she had to check that it would pass muster with the Germans.

It was the right colour, beige with a navy border, and dog-eared despite its leather protection. A bland black and white photo, the duty-paid stamp, two fingerprints in bright purple ink, both official stamps in the right places, an ink blot in the bottom left hand corner — it all looked reassuringly authentic, and Aliénor's anxiety eased. According to the document he was Peter Laval, a factory worker born in Strasbourg in 1918, with an address in Poitiers, one metre eighty-eight tall, brown hair, no moustache, blue eyes, a straight average-sized nose and oval face.

She frowned. 'You're not working? That's not very likely.' Labour was scarce, and there was a job for every able-bodied man.

'I'm on my way to the Atlantic coast. They need workers there to help build up the fortifications.'

He had his answer off pat. Aliénor nodded, satisfied. It sounded plausible. One other detail gave her some concern, and she frowned again.

'You've given your first name as Peter. But it's your real name.'

He bent, picked up a stone and with a vicious sweep of his arm, sent it skimming over the top of the vines. 'And why not?' Aliénor could hear the anger in his voice. With a shock, she understood that the days of sunshine combined with his enforced inactivity had lulled her into forgetting he was first and foremost a combatant. 'Yes, it's my own name. If I'm fighting in a foreign country, it's important to me to fight under my own name.'

*　*　*

She was avid for knowledge about him, and like a miner sifting for gold she hoarded the nuggets of information that came her way:

He'd been an engineer in civvy street.

He lived somewhere south of London, but his grandmother was Swiss and as a child he'd often spent the summer holidays with her. That was how he spoke such good French.

His mother was a concert pianist and his father had a factory that manufactured pianos, and that was how they'd met.

He had three sisters, all older than him, making him the adored baby of the family.

She pictured a cheerful, easy-going family. So different from her own life, bounded by formality and lacking in love, she thought with a pang.

* * *

Another day, and they sat on the bench outside the hut again. The vines nearby stood at head-height, rangy and wild, and lush with slowly ripening fruit.

'What you do couldn't be more dangerous, could it?' She kept returning to the reason for his presence in her country, the danger inherent in what he did, picking at her fears like a child picking at a festering scab.

'It's my job. I show other people how

to blow up bridges and railway lines. That's what I do. In fact it is safe. Here — ' She'd asked him to show her the tools of his trade and he'd come out of the hut with a canvas bag which he placed on the bench between them. He held out a small cylinder of something wrapped in waxed paper. 'Hold it. Go on.'

She looked at him before taking it and reading the writing on the packaging: Nobel's Explosive no. 808. She pressed it cautiously between thumb and forefinger. It gave slightly, like putty or plasticine. She brought it up to her nose. It smelt of almonds.

'Before it can go off, it needs a detonator. One of these.' He held up a silver object about the size and shape of a cigarette. 'And this is a time pencil.' It indeed looked like a pencil, though a little longer and thicker, and made of copper and aluminium. 'See the black band round it? That means there's a ten-minute delay before it sets the detonator off.'

'And that's what went wrong.' There was a catch in her voice as she remembered the dreadful injuries he'd suffered. She handed the packet of explosive back. All at once she wanted nothing more to do with it.

'What happened was a fluke. A freak accident. It was a warm night. If anything, I'd have expected it to go off *before* it was supposed to.'

'What's to stop it happening again?' She wanted to tell him not to do it anymore, not to put himself in danger anymore, but of course she couldn't.

'Mélisande, my dear.' He stood up, bringing her to her feet and gathering her into his arms. 'What can I say to reassure you? Sometimes things go wrong. We have to take risks. But we're fighting a war against a vile enemy. We have no choice.'

Another afternoon, full of sun. As they walked between the rows of vines, he took her hand in his, and awareness whispered along the skin of her arm.

'What about you, my sweet Mélisande?' he asked. 'How did you get mixed up in all this?'

And her thoughts went back to the day in March that had started it all.

* * *

As she often did, she'd been visiting people on the estate who were in difficulty of one sort or another. That afternoon there had been Berthe, old and lonely and starting to lose her mind to senility; Juliette, who had borne a child out of wedlock and had been cast off by her family; and Lionel and Albertine, resolutely independent but too old now to tend their land and care for their animals. To these people Aliénor brought company, food if possible, and help. She knew it wasn't enough, though. It was never enough.

She'd cycled down the lane that led to her final destination, Suzanne's farmhouse, frowning when she saw that the tall double gates and the side gate, usually kept open, were both shut.

Propping her bicycle against the wall, she knocked at the side gate. 'Suzanne, it's me, Aliénor,' she called.

There was no reply. An uneasy stillness hovered. Then she heard voices, faint, quietly frantic. The hairs at the back of Aliénor's neck lifted.

She knocked louder, called again, pressed the gate's latch down. It wouldn't open. She looked round, unsure what to do next, when to her immense relief she heard the clatter of clogs from the courtyard side of the gate and the sound of the bar that kept the side gate closed being lifted. It swung open.

Suzanne stood before her, stick-thin, one hand holding the latch of the gate, the other cupping her stomach, which already looked too painfully large for her small body. The faded cotton wraparound apron she wore over her jersey and skirt did little to disguise her condition. Five-year-old Jérôme stood behind his mother, partially hidden behind her skirt. Huge eyes stared up at her from his pale face. But it was the expression on Suzanne's face, wary and afraid, that gave Aliénor pause.

'What's the matter?' she asked, trying to hide her shock. 'Is it the baby?'

A shake of the head, the eyes watchful, guarded.

'I've brought you some food,' Aliénor said. It was the cruel time of year when the garden produced little and winter stores were low or had run out. Suzanne and Jérôme's staple diet at the moment consisted of potatoes and Jerusalem artichokes.

She took a cotton bag from the wicker basket that hung from the handlebars of her bicycle. It contained eggs and half a goat's cheese. 'Here,' she said, and was appalled to see silent tears coursing down the other woman's face. 'There *is* something wrong, Suzanne.' She moved forward into the courtyard, setting the bag down on the ground — carefully; the food was precious — and put her arm round

Suzanne's shoulders, gently turning her round. 'Come on, let's go in and sit you down.'

'No, we can't — '

'Yes we can. Jérôme *chéri*,' she called behind her. 'Bring the bag in, will you.'

It was dark inside, and Aliénor paused on the threshold to give her eyes time to adjust. A shadowy movement from the direction of the fireplace combined with the tension that gripped Suzanne's body warned her someone else was there. She looked up, pulses racing.

A man stood in front of the fireplace. Round black-framed glasses gave him a bookish air, but his expression was fierce, his stance aggressive. One hand hovered near the fire-tongs, ready to seize them. He wasn't a German. At least, Aliénor corrected herself, he wasn't in uniform. His dark jacket and trousers looked too loose for him, as though made for better-fed days.

'I told you not to let anyone in,' the man snarled.

With a sob, Suzanne wrenched herself away from Aliénor's arms. 'I'm sorry. I — I didn't know what to do.' She stood, wretched with misery, midway between Aliénor and the man. 'She's from the château. She — '

'The Château de la Tour Dragondas? What on earth are you thinking of? That place is crawling with Germans.' He was definitely French. Both his accent and his derisive tone confirmed it.

'It's all right, Patrice. You can trust her. Please.'

Aliénor sensed the man's aggression was no more than a mask to hide his fear. Even so, her mouth was dry, her own fear ready to blaze into anger. 'Is he — ?'

She took a step forward, directing her remark at Suzanne, her glance going to the other woman's stomach. From the corner of her eye she saw Jérôme sidle into the room, the bag of food cradled in his arms.

'No.'

She looked over at the man and kept her voice neutral, not wanting to provoke him. 'You're right, my home is crawling with Germans as you put it, but I certainly didn't invite them there.'

The man shifted slightly. 'You're friendly with them. Everyone says so.'

'I see no point in antagonising people unnecessarily. But I don't like them and I want them out of my country.' She met his gaze with a calm she was far from feeling and was relieved when he appeared to come to a decision, his shoulders relaxing a fraction. 'Who are you?' she asked.

'He's my cousin from Tours.' Suzanne's voice shook as she wiped her eyes on the skirt of her apron.

The young man hesitated. 'Patrice Lebel.' He put out his hand and Aliénor reached forward, giving it a single quick shake. He was wary still, but so was she.

'Aliénor Rochefontaine de Montfort. So why have you come here? What's going on?'

131

'The new law. I'm twenty-two. I'm supposed to register for the compulsory work programme. But I refuse to be sent to Germany.' He looked at her, eyes narrowing as if debating some issue. When he opened his mouth to speak, Aliénor knew instinctively he'd made the decision to trust her. 'I intend joining the Resistance.'

He spoke with quiet intensity. There was no reaction from Suzanne or her son. They were murmuring to each other excitedly, busy taking the food she'd brought out of the bag and stacking it on a shelf. Clearly they already knew what Patrice intended. Or thought it best not to know.

Aliénor too was making a decision. She didn't question it. It was simply the natural, the obvious thing to do. She thought about the people she knew who never had enough to eat, about those whose men folk were missing, and about the petty bureaucratic restrictions everyone endured every day. Minor irritations, perhaps, when compared to being wounded or killed in battle. But very real and a constant low-level trial nonetheless. One person was powerless to do much, but acting together . . .

'I can be useful to you.' As he had done with her, she was going to put her trust in this serious, intense man only a few years older than herself. 'Let me help you.'

To her relief, he saw her potential straight away. She lived among German soldiers, important ones too: a general and two other officers. She understood a fair amount of German, and the officers spoke good French. She'd be in a position to pass on all sorts of valuable information to the Resistance.

'There's a group in the Scévolles forest,' he said finally. 'I'm going down there to make contact. I'll leave tonight.'

'Keep me informed.'

They shook hands again, and this time all wariness had gone. They were allies now in the fight against the army that occupied their country.

A week later she'd gone back to Suzanne's farmhouse, taking more food than usual, for Patrice too had to be fed.

'They want me to stay somewhere near you so I can pass messages from you to them,' Patrice had told her.

Aliénor frowned. 'Not here, though. It's too dangerous for Suzanne. I know just the place. I'll take you to it.'

So they'd gathered some provisions and rolled up a couple of blankets. While Patrice wheeled out the bicycle that had belonged to Suzanne's husband, Aliénor said goodbye to the young woman and her son, and they set off for the abandoned grape-pickers' hut and vineyard enclosed by woods on three sides. It was primitive in the extreme. It had no water or sanitation, but there was a spring close by, and Patrice could dig a latrine in the wood. Cooking and keeping warm were more of a problem. There was no electricity, of course — the grid hadn't reached remote farmhouses and hamlets in the area — and the smoke from a log fire would betray his presence to the Germans.

'You must try and forget what my real name is. Call me 'Christian' from now on. They've given you a codename too. 'Mélisande'.'

As Aliénor came to the end of her story, she looked at Peter. Unease whispered like a cool breath across her skin, and she pulled her hand away from his. Mélisande, the character in the opera, had been married to someone but had fallen in love with someone else.

But it was a codename, chosen at random by a person she didn't know. So why should she now feel uneasy?

8

It was about five in the afternoon a few days later when Aliénor cycled down past the south wing of the château. From behind her on the right came the murmur of voices on the terrace. She caught her mother's tinkling laugh, men's laughter too, and the chink of glasses. From further away came the tramping of many feet, shouted orders, the revving of an engine.

Aliénor was about to turn towards the outbuilding where she stored her bicycle when a flash of colour on the lawn in front of her stopped her. She gave a gasp of delight. A pair of hoopoes, their honey-pink bodies and black and white wings and tails a bright contrast to the green of the grass, were probing the soil with their long slender bills.

One of the pair pulled out a fat white

grub, and Aliénor's mouth formed a silent 'oh' of wonder as it crossed the lawn and fed the grub to its mate. It was a magical sight, and she stood transfixed, the noise of marching men far, far away. Even the sounds of laughter from the terrace and the curiously irregular rhythm of someone walking close by couldn't detract from the enchantment of the scene.

'Here you are at last, *mademoiselle*.'

A German voice speaking good French. A voice she'd heard before but couldn't place. The hackles rose along her spine, and she spun round. A tall man, stern in his grey Gestapo uniform, stood before her, some two metres away. He held his cap and a walking stick in his left hand. An ugly scar, vivid red against his pale skin, ran in a straight line from chin to temple. She didn't recognise him at first. Then her eyes widened in shock. Hot colour flooded her cheeks, writing her guilt all over her face.

'Colonel Ostermeyer.' Her skin crawled

with the danger of it. She'd hurried through her estate duties and had spent most of the day up at the hut with Peter. If she gave the Gestapo colonel even the slightest hint of where she'd been, who she'd been with, he'd arrest her in a trice. The consequences — for her, for Christian and the Englishman, for the burgeoning local resistance net-work — didn't bear thinking about.

Behind her, she heard the flap of wings as the two birds took flight. The magic was lost, and anger flared, swiftly suppressed as she wiped all expression, all show of emotion from her face. 'If I'd known we were expecting guests, I'd have been back earlier.'

She met his gaze with a confidence she didn't feel, and saw the hint of a smile play across his lips.

'Walk with me, *mademoiselle*.'

It was an order, not a request. She looked across to the terrace. Her mother stood close to the balustrade, away from the others. Glass in hand, beautiful in a full-length lilac gown, she'd been watching the two of them. With a nod to her daughter, she turned back to her guests.

No help there. Aliénor's thoughts were in turmoil. Why had the colonel come back to the château? The acting director of the French Propaganda Department — why had he sought her out? Because he suspected she was connected with the Resistance? Her thoughts flew to Christian and the Englishman. She mustn't betray even a glimmer of what she knew.

She turned back to the colonel. 'Very well,' she said with a gracious smile.

Crossing the two metres between them, Ostermeyer took the bicycle from her and propped it against a tree. He moved with a pronounced limp, the walking stick taking the force of his weight, and her thoughts went back to the afternoon he and Théodore Gaillard had left the château. She'd told Christian where the Gestapo colonel and his men were going next. Had the Resistance ambushed them? Were his limp and the scar on his face the result?

Braced for some kind of interrogation to start straight away, Aliénor was disconcerted when they walked in silence for a while, side by side, following a path that skirted the lake before turning into the trees on their left. The sun was warm on her skin, but inside she was cold with a wary fear. The Gestapo colonel's expression was one of grim determination. Whether that was due to the effort required for walking, or for some other reason, she couldn't tell.

As they reached the trees, a blackbird called out in alarm, swooping away low through the branches. The path was uneven here, and Ostermeyer slipped, wincing, on a stone.

'Am I allowed to ask what happened to you?' Aliénor said, seizing the opportunity to break the silence. Her nerves were on edge. The strain of not speaking, not knowing anything, had become too much.

'I'd have been disappointed if you

hadn't asked.' He took a silver cigarette case out of his jacket pocket. 'Cigarette?'

'No, thanks. I don't smoke.' Anxiety gnawed at her. How was she to interpret his remark?

Pocketing his lighter, he drew deeply on his cigarette before moving off again. 'I got two bullets in the leg. One a flesh wound, but the other clipped the thigh-bone. The third sliced across my face. As you can see.' He spoke coldly, without emotion.

Aliénor's thoughts raced. What questions would he expect her to ask in response? Or should she keep silent? Fear of saying the wrong thing urged her to caution. She ran her tongue round dry lips. 'I'm sorry.'

Ostermeyer looked at her, his sardonic smile and the inclination of his head acknowledging the lie.

A hundred or so metres further on, he stopped, crushing his cigarette against the trunk of a tree, and turned to face her. The knuckles of his left hand were taut and white across the handle of his walking stick, and lines of pain were etched into his features. Even so, Aliénor couldn't find it in her heart to feel sympathy for this man, then scolded herself for her lack of womanly feelings.

'You are remarkably incurious today, *mademoiselle*.'

Aliénor's stomach lurched, fear spilling over into anger with herself. She'd made the wrong choice. 'You're forgetting,' she said. 'For the last three years it's been drummed into me not to ask questions, not to — '

He smiled, and she caught herself up with a jolt. Was that his game? she thought furiously. To goad her into saying something indiscreet — or worse?

He stepped forward a pace. 'It happened the day after we left here. An ambush. Gaillard and two of my men were killed.' He was close now. Too close. She could see the bristles of the next day's beard, as blond as his hair.

She could see every dent and trough in that ugly scar. She could smell cigarette smoke and soap. A sick panic welled. What should she do? What *could* she do?

'My last evening here,' he went on, leaning heavily on his walking stick. 'Do you remember? Out on the terrace.' His other hand came up, stroking across her cheek and on into her hair. Aliénor opened her mouth. She wanted to push him away. She'd never expected this. But something, the intensity of his voice perhaps, kept her silent, and her hands fell back.

'All day, every day, I'm surrounded by yes-men,' he said. His fingers pushed further into her hair, leaving tingling trails along her scalp. His touch was insistent, strangely compelling, a bitter-sweet caress. 'You — ' He gave a slight emphasis to the pronoun. ' — were a refreshing change.'

She could have taken a step back, freeing herself. But she didn't, and all at once she was aware of every tiny woodland sound — the rustle of leaves, the sighing of branches as they moved in the breeze. Apart from the whisper of his breath, and hers, not a single human noise intruded. It was as if he'd cast a spell on her, and something awakened deep inside her.

His fingers tangled in her hair, drawing her ever closer, and she found her voice at last. 'Don't. I — '

The movement of his hand stilled at once. She thought she saw regret cross his face. 'Don't, because you are engaged to be married to the delightful Henri d'Eparnelle.' His fingers twisted as they slid down all the length of her hair. 'I wish you joy of him.'

'Henri, yes.' She seized on the name although, in truth, she rarely thought of him. Their marriage seemed very distant. She swallowed hard. Her voice was choked with emotion. 'We must go back. My mother will be wondering where I am.'

'Of course.' He pulled out his cigarette case and lit a cigarette, and they started back to the château. Aliénor found she was trembling. He was the enemy. A colonel in the Gestapo. One of their top people. How could she have even let him touch her?

They came out of the trees and on to the path. She could hear laughter from the terrace, and music. Someone must have brought the gramophone player out.

Ostermeyer threw his cigarette down. 'You haven't said where you've been all day.'

Aliénor's heart stopped for an instant before swooping into a rapid, shallow beat. So that was how he did it — played with his victim first, then pounced.

'I — uh — ' Her voice shook. She cleared her throat, began again. 'Seeing various people on the estate.' Her chin came up. 'Do you want me to list them for you?'

'That won't be necessary.'

They'd arrived at the foot of the steps which led up to the terrace. The gramophone was playing a German marching song. Several of the guests were singing along. The local wine that was all the château could offer was clearly having its effect.

Ostermeyer turned to face her. 'It's not a good idea to be wandering the countryside when communist saboteurs are on the loose.'

'But you're after them, aren't you? So they won't be on the loose for long.'

He didn't reply straight away. Then: 'As outspoken as ever, *mademoiselle*.' He spoke quietly, but she sensed the simmering anger behind the neutral tone, and her heart gave a painful thump. She'd gone too far. His right hand touched under her chin, tilting it up, forcing her to look into his eyes, cold and hard as stone. 'Be careful, Aliénor.' The warning was unmistakable. 'It'll get you into trouble one of these days.'

She watched, dry-mouthed, as he turned and made his way awkwardly up the steps to the terrace. Leaning back against the wall, she closed her eyes. She was trembling all over. A cold, hollow fear churned in her stomach, but her relief knew no bounds. She'd survived. She hadn't betrayed the two brave men who fought to free her country. *A prisoner who's been given a reprieve must feel like this*, she thought shakily. She shivered despite the sun's warmth, and forced herself to take slow, calming breaths in an effort to still her racing pulse.

'Aliénor.' It was her mother, her voice light and sparkling, calling from the top of the steps. 'Come on up.'

Aliénor stiffened as she came away from the wall and climbed the steps. At the top she stopped and faced her mother. There was wariness in Thérèse's smile, bright for the benefit of her guests, and in the eyes that searched her daughter's features.

'Why?' Aliénor asked, directing her fear and confusion — unfairly, she knew — in an angry accusation at her mother. Laughter, loud male voices and the music from the gramophone, another marching song, meant no one could hear them. 'You're supposed to protect me. Keep me safe until my marriage.'

Her mother paled, her eyes dropping to her hands, clasped tightly to her stomach. She twisted her wedding ring round and round. The scent from the posy of lavender and pansies she wore pinned to her gown surrounded her in the still air. 'He assured me he meant you no harm,' she murmured.

'What?' Bewildered, she looked across at Colonel Ostermeyer, who was sinking into an armchair over by the balustrade, his leg sticking out stiffly in front of him. Two other Gestapo officers were at his side, one offering him a cigarette, the other lighting it for him. The colonel took a sip from his glass and tilted his head, all his concentration fixed on what they were telling him.

Aliénor's anger drained from her, and she felt a stab of pity for her mother.

She'd had no choice. A request from a Gestapo colonel was a thinly veiled command. Once again, Aliénor was reminded that her parents lived on a knife's edge. One wrong move and they could lose everything. Their home, their lands — their daughter.

'It's all right, *mère*. Nothing happened.' Her hand came up to pat Thérèse's arm, but she let it fall back to her side. Her mother didn't welcome such familiarity. 'I'm tired. I'm going to my room.'

Thérèse made no protest as she moved past her. Aliénor saw Ralf standing stony-faced with Major Kellner and General Hartmann some distance from the two groups of Gestapo officers. He came away from his two fellow officers, long purposeful strides bringing him fast across the terrace to stand in her way. Anger towards her rolled off him in waves.

'You're a fool. He's got a mistress in Paris.'

Aliénor recoiled. Ralf's words were

like a slap round the face. She blinked, fighting back the tears. He was the one German she cared about. She didn't want to lose his goodwill.

'Well, good for him,' she said, 'because he hasn't got one here.' With a sob, she pushed through the doors and into the château.

★　★　★

Peter stooped to pick up a third feather, three shades of grey this time, a pigeon's feather, and added it to the two rook's feathers he already held, black and velvet-soft like the night.

'You're making a collection?' she asked, happy simply to be walking at his side along one of the woodland paths near the grape-pickers' hut. She couldn't take her eyes off him; loved watching the play of light and shade thrown by the leaves of the trees across his face.

Colonel Ostermeyer had left with his men some time the day before. She didn't know when exactly. After their encounter in the château grounds, she hadn't seen him again.

'This chap Weyland the Smith,' he said, twirling the feathers between his fingers, 'was imprisoned on an island. He gathered feathers, lots of them, fashioned them into wings and flew away.'

'Like Icarus.' All of a sudden she was cold, as if the sun had gone in behind a cloud. 'Is that how *you* feel? Imprisoned — trapped — here?' Her voice was husky. She couldn't bear it if that was how he felt.

He came to a halt, the feathers dropping to the ground as one hand caught her waist, swinging her round to face him. He brought his other hand to her chin, tilting it up towards him. 'No, Mélisande, sweetheart. No, that's not what I meant. But one day soon, I too am going to have to fly away.'

'How soon?' She could hardly trust herself to speak. A yawning emptiness stretched before her. How could she live without him?

'One month. Two. I don't know exactly. There'll be a message for me from the radio operator in Scévolles forest. Christian'll get it to me.'

'I don't want you to go.' Her voice shook. She was conscious of his hands against her back.

'I don't want to go either. But I'm afraid I'll have no choice in the matter.' His voice, like hers, held a rough edge, and Aliénor had to blink back her tears. 'Don't cry, my dear,' he said, and his hands slid from her back, coming up to cup her face.

She closed her eyes as his face drew nearer hers. He kissed each eyelid in turn and a shiver sped through her. Her hands found his neck, fingers pushing up, tangling with his hair, and she trembled when he touched kisses, each a feather-light caress, to her forehead, cheeks and nose. She brushed her fingertips over the bristles of his jaw line, marvelling at the contrast with her own smooth skin.

With a sound something like a groan, he brought his hands up to her shoulder-blades, crushing her to him. His lips found hers, and all at once she was melting, melting into the curves of his body, held in the firm grip of his arms, and she gave herself over to the desperate joy of that long lingering kiss.

★   ★   ★

Three days later and they walked in single file along a narrow path through the forest. Aliénor led the way, setting an easy pace but moving with purpose. She knew exactly where she was going, knew what she had to say. And already it was as if her heart was breaking.

Over a month had passed since he was injured, over a month since he'd come into her life, and Peter had regained his strength and health. The injury to his scalp had healed well, as had the wound on his leg, although the shiny pink scar that ran in a jagged line down the side of his calf would stay with him, possibly for years. Aliénor had cycled up to the hut every day she could. At first she'd told herself it was to make sure the Englishman's recovery was progressing as it should. She had no intention of getting involved with him. She knew where her duty lay. A few days spent in his company would do no harm, though, would it? she'd reassured herself as the days slipped into weeks.

But it wasn't long before she knew that she could fool herself no more. In the dark hours of the night when her mind reran the events of each previous day, the things they'd talked about, the way he took her into his arms with that easy familiarity she found so beguiling, that assured touch that made her skin sing, she'd been forced to recognise, deep inside, that he'd become an obsession. A fever in her blood.

And it had to stop. There could be no future in any relationship between the two of them. She didn't know what *his* feelings for *her* were. She couldn't ask him. It wasn't something a young lady did. Perhaps he was always hugging her to him, kissing her hair, her nose, her lips, because he came from a family that wore its heart on its sleeve. Or he was simply expressing the gratitude of a patient towards his nurse. Or, perhaps — perhaps his feelings for her ran deeper.

With a determined shake of her head, she pushed a springy bramble aside, holding it carefully between thumb and index finger, and glanced behind her to make sure he'd seen it.

'So where are you taking me, fair Mélisande?' he asked, taking the bramble stem from her and holding it back so that he too could pass.

She smiled, a bittersweet smile of happiness now and pain to come. She loved to hear that teasing note in his voice; would hear it no more after today. 'You'll see. We're almost there.'

A while back, they'd passed close by the spring she called her own, and now they moved along a path that wove its way uphill through the woodland. And at last they were there.

It was a spot where the ground fell sharply before easing into a gentler slope thick with trees and bushes. They stood on the cliff edge, screened from any watcher by the vertical stems of an elder. Large clusters of berries, not yet ripe, hung from the higher branches, rich food later in the year for the creatures of the forest. Peter stood behind her and she was glad. It would make things easier if she couldn't see his face. She was achingly aware, though, of the gentle pressure of his hands round her upper arms and his chin on the top of her head. But she wouldn't move away, not just yet, she thought, breathing in the salt tang of his skin.

'That's quite a view,' he said.

She'd brought him to the south side of the château. Rising less than a kilometre away, its limestone walls, in the shape of a letter c with squared corners, gleamed a shimmering white in the sunlight. The formal gardens, driveways and paths that girdled the building gave way before long to wilder land, and further away still, to forest broken in places by wall-edged fields. It was a lush fertile corner of France even in the heat of these summer months, the signs of military activity by the north wing of the château — vehicles on the move and a column of marching men — failing to detract from the beauty of the place. As her heart swelled with pride, Aliénor could forget for a moment why she stood there on the cliff edge.

'The Château de la Tour Dragondas,' she said, just loud enough for him to hear. 'It's my family home. My family has lived here for more than a thousand years. We own most of what you can see: the château and its grounds, the forest, the fields and the farmhouses, that village over there.' There were other farms, hamlets and villages that belonged to the estate but they were out of sight.

'Go on.' She thought she detected a grim edge to his even, carefully neutral tone.

'Mélisande is my codename of course. My real name is Aliénor Rochefontaine de Montfort.' She paused and swallowed before ploughing on, willing the shakiness out of her voice. 'I'm engaged to be married to — '

She sensed him stiffen, felt the loss as he lifted his chin from her head, the grip of his hands round her arms tightening the barest fraction, and she faltered to a halt.

'Who? Who are you engaged to?'

'Henri d'Eparnelle. He's — '

'This is crazy. You don't — you can't — love him.' He growled the words, making them a flat statement of fact, allowing for no contradiction.

He was right, she knew that now. 'Love will come,' she said tonelessly.

'Look at me.' His hands fell away from her arms and she turned round. Wretchedly she scanned the taut lines of his face. His cheeks had lost their colour, the expression in his eyes dark and unreadable. 'So you're telling me that you're spoken for? Is that it?'

'Yes.' It hurt to speak. 'I can't go on seeing you. I won't be coming back up to the hut. Not until you've gone back to England.'

His jaw jerked up as if she'd punched him. 'You don't love him. You can't marry someone you don't love.' She could hear the anger that rippled beneath the surface of his words.

'I've already made the commitment. It's my duty.'

He must have heard the misery in her voice, for all at once she was in his arms. One hand held her against his chest, the other stroked her hair. 'Mélisande, my dearest, my sweet, only kings and queens, princes and princesses marry out of duty.'

She shook her head. She couldn't tell him that her reason for marrying Henri was to bring much-needed money into the family. 'Please,' she said. 'Don't make it any harder.'

He stilled, pushed her gently away, cupping her elbows, and looked into her eyes. Then he looked over her shoulder, staring beyond her at the view of the château and the vast estate that surrounded it.

'The habits and customs of an old aristocratic French family, still stuck in the nineteenth century. I can't fight that, can I?' He spoke as much to himself as to her, his voice low and harsh with the bitter anger of resignation. 'I must accept what you say.' For a long, long moment he said nothing, his gaze moving over her face in a soft caress. 'Look, will you be able to find your way back to the hut all right? To collect your bike?' He spoke quietly, gently, and his tenderness was somehow worse than if he'd been bitingly angry. 'I rather think I need to stay here by myself for a while.'

She could only nod, didn't trust herself to speak.

'Sure?' he asked.

Again she could only nod. This was

what heartbreak was, she thought: a swelling ache in heart and throat and face, an infinite sadness, painful beyond belief; and she wasn't sure she could bear it.

He bent to touch a kiss to her lips. 'You'll always be 'Mélisande' for me. I can't think of you by any other name.' Another kiss, feather-light, achingly tender. 'Farewell, my own sweet Mélisande,' he said, and the gruffness in his voice told her he shared her pain.

★   ★   ★

He filled her mind. She couldn't stop thinking about him. She touched stone walls, rough and sun-warmed, and she was touching him. She heard the growl of a dog, the purr of a cat, a man's soft voice, and she heard him. She saw in the distance a tall, slim, dark-haired man, and she saw him. She tasted the salt of her tears, and she tasted his skin.

And she would never see him again.

9

Suzanne was sitting in a straight-backed chair by the window, suckling her baby, when Aliénor came into the kitchen. The room was filled with the rich smell of coffee made from chicory, keeping warm in the hearth. With a gasp of alarm, Suzanne half-rose out of her seat. 'Have you heard something? Is it bad news?'

'Heard? I haven't heard anything. What are you talking about?' Anxiety made her harsh. After a sleepless anguish-ridden night, she'd decided the solution was to keep busy, so busy that all thoughts of Peter would be banished from her mind. Hence the visit to Suzanne, even as she recognised the contradiction: being Christian's cousin meant that Suzanne was a continuing link, however tenuous, with Peter.

Had he flown back to England during the night? Was that what Suzanne somehow knew about? Her Peter hundreds of kilometres away, in another country, separated by an uncrossable sea of water? More finally lost to her than ever?

'Tell me what you know, Suzanne, please.' Crossing the room, she pulled out a chair and sat down across the table from the other woman.

The baby hiccupped and Suzanne smiled, all her concentration on her baby as she cradled her to her chest, lightly stroking her dark hair with the tips of her fingers. She was thriving on motherhood, Aliénor thought with an unaccountable pang.

'I don't know anything. Just that they'll be gone for three days.'

'They?' Aliénor found she was holding her breath.

'Christian and — well, you'll know more about the other man than I do.'

Peter. It had to be Peter, not some

other Resistance colleague of Christian's. Aliénor's heart gave an irrational leap of joy that he was still somewhere nearby. Then a shiver of fear flickered down her spine. This surely meant he was resuming operations.

Three days, or rather, three nights. One to get there, cycling through the night, avoiding towns, villages, German patrols. One to do the job, blowing up a bridge or a railway line. The third to get back, hastened along by the knowledge that the German military would be actively hunting them. He and Christian must be there now, at their destination, hiding up somewhere, sleeping in the day, ready to sabotage their small part of the German war machine in the shadows of the coming night.

Fear for him, for them both, spread like a poison through her blood. 'Three days. So they'll be back Friday.' Friday the thirteenth, she thought sickly, and barely heard the clatter of clogs from outside.

Suzanne smiled as her son came running in. He was followed by a man Aliénor hadn't met before. In his late forties, she thought, he wore loose trousers that were belted at the waist and a collarless shirt open at the neck, the sleeves rolled up above the elbows. A cigarette made from some foul-smelling ersatz tobacco stuck to his lower lip.

'This is Georges,' Suzanne said. There was pride in her voice. 'He's been sent to work on the farm.'

The man shook Aliénor's hand and murmured a greeting before crossing to Suzanne. 'Hmm, coffee smells good.' He stood behind her, massaging her shoulders with his solid countryman's hands. 'Hungry?'

Suzanne turned her head to send him a slow shy smile. 'Yes.'

It was a smile full of secrets, that answered more than the simple question. He was almost certainly the baby's father, Aliénor thought, and something like envy twisted inside her. She turned to five-year-old Jérôme who stood solemnly beside her, waiting for her kiss.

'We're having breakfast now, *mademoiselle*,' the boy said. His face was pinched still but had taken on some outdoor colour. 'Would you like some?'

Breakfast? Aliénor kissed him, looked at her wrist, and saw she'd forgotten to put her watch on. It had to be eight o'clock or so, possibly even earlier. No wonder Suzanne had been so alarmed when she'd first arrived.

She smiled at Jérôme. 'That's very kind of you, *mon ange*.' It was an effort to force the words out. 'But no thank you. I must be going.' Standing up, she made her farewells and left the farmhouse kitchen. She was pleased for Suzanne, she really was. A woman needed a man, a protector, especially in these dangerous times. But it made her aware, even more acutely than before, of her own self-imposed loss.

★ ★ ★

Back at the château, Aliénor went straight to her room. She didn't want breakfast; couldn't face the thought of food. She sat on her bed, stood up, paced, sat in the armchair by the window with the view over the woodland and tree-covered hills that she'd always loved so much, stood up again, and paced some more in an endless, restless cycle. And all the time, her fear sped on like a motor racing out of control. What if he were lying dead somewhere? Or dying slowly in a pool of blood in a place where she wasn't there to care for him? What if he'd been captured and they were even now pulling his fingernails out? A cry of anguish rose, and she stuffed her fingers in her mouth, shutting her eyes against the dreadful images.

Her one consolation, she thought as she cycled to Suzanne's farmhouse the following Friday — later in the morning than her previous visit — was that the soldiers at the château had stayed put, had kept to their normal routines.

There had been no alarms, no indication that the hunt was on for the man they called the Smith.

'Christian came by before sunrise this morning.' Suzanne sat on a chair outside in the sun, nursing her daughter, while her son played nearby. There was no sign of Georges. 'He's fine. His companion too, I think. I didn't see him, mind. He stayed out of sight.'

Aliénor's relief was immense. He was safe. Peter was back safe, that was all that mattered.

'They're off again on Monday,' Suzanne added, and Aliénor's whole body grew tense. All at once her mouth was dry, and she knew there would be no let-up to her fear for the man she'd lost.

She didn't know how she got through the days. And the nights when she lay turning restlessly in an agony of grief at her loss, fear for his safety, were worse, far worse. But she knew she'd have to pull herself together the morning at breakfast, soon after, that her mother gave her a long keen-eyed look. Aliénor knew what her mother was seeing. She recalled her shock that morning when she caught her reflection in the mirror while cleaning her teeth. How thin her face had become, how bruised-looking her eyes.

'You're looking peaky, Aliénor,' her mother said.

'I haven't been sleeping,' Aliénor replied, in partial truth at least, and added the lie, 'It's the heat during the night. It's stifling.' She spread a film of jam over the slice of bread on her plate, took a mouthful, chewed and swallowed. It felt like a large indigestible lump as it went down but had the desired effect: her mother watched her closely for a second or two longer, gave a nod of approval and returned to her own breakfast.

Those first days set the pattern for the days that followed. Suzanne became her intermediary, her only way of having some indication at least of how

169

Peter was faring. But of course the other woman could only tell her *when* he went away. She wasn't told where, or what the target was. The two men would spend several nights on an operation, and a day or two at the hut to recover before leaving on the next one. He was setting a frantic, almost dangerous, pace, Aliénor thought, worry churning her stomach, making up perhaps for the time he'd lost recuperating from his injuries.

She became adept at disguising her fear for him, from her mother in particular, but also from the soldiers at the château; from any watching eyes in fact. For her mother's benefit she forced herself to eat, while sheer exhaustion, emotional rather than physical, helped give her much-needed sleep. Her face filled out again, her eyes lost their shadows, and no one could guess how much she yearned for a return of those lazy days, which seemed so long ago now, when he'd been safe and had held her in his arms.

The fifteenth of August and it was Aliénor's birthday. Wartime restrictions, on travel and food especially, meant her parents kept it a small affair. She didn't mind at all. She didn't feel like celebrating anything.

The month was nearing its close when she glimpsed Ralf walking in the distance by himself. He was so rarely alone that this was an opportunity too good to be missed. She headed for the trees, hoping to intercept him as if by chance somewhere near the lake.

Though the days were hot still, the sky clear blue and cloudless, there was a slight chill in the early-evening air, hinting at the end of summer. Children would be returning to school soon, and young Jérôme would be starting at the village primary. It was a time of sadness and of new beginnings, but she was aware only of the sadness. When she saw two rook's feathers lying on the path she was taking through the trees, she almost turned back to the sanctuary of her room.

Ralf stood near the edge of the lake, close to the reed bed, reading a letter. Hearing her approach, he looked up, folded the sheet of light blue paper in two, and pushed it into the breast pocket of his uniform jacket. His smile was bleak as he took his cap off in greeting.

'Bad news?' Aliénor asked. Her concern was genuine. His brother had been fighting in Russia, and his family had heard nothing from him for eight long months.

He sighed as he replaced his cap. 'No news. And that's just as bad.'

Worse, Aliénor thought, but didn't say. At least she knew, via Suzanne, each time Peter and Christian returned safely to the grape-pickers' hut.

They stood side by side, both silent, gazing out across the lake. Unseen creatures caused rings of water to ripple outwards, the occasional 'plop' the only sound close by. The noise of military activity from further away was nothing but a muted background in the still air.

Uncertain how to bring the subject round to what she wanted to know, Aliénor glanced over at the château. Her parents were on the terrace, having a pre-dinner glass of wine, no doubt keeping an eye on her and the German captain.

She turned back to Ralf. 'At least it's quiet around here,' she ventured. 'Not like Russia.'

'It is.' His sigh was heavy. 'Otto certainly drew the short straw.'

She put her hand on his sleeve. 'I'm sorry, Ralf. I really am.' She hesitated. 'I overheard a man in Loudun say you were looking for someone called the Smith.'

He stiffened. It was as if she'd touched a raw nerve.

'Curiosity is the devil's work, isn't that what you French say?' His voice was hard, his expression grim, and sweat pricked out under Aliénor's arms.

'It's a bit of a paraphrase,' she said, 'but yes, I suppose so. Anatole France said it.'

He took her hands in his. Warm, expressive hands. Like Peter's. The thought came unbidden, and she looked down, closing her eyes against the pain. Would it always be like this? Would she never stop thinking of him?

Ralf gave her hands a shake and she looked up.

'I don't often agree with Colonel Ostermeyer, Aliénor, but he's correct about one thing.' His voice softened a fraction. 'If you know what's good for you, you must, you really must, watch what you say.' He paused, and she nodded, unable to speak, touched by his concern — and the coded warning. 'Let me take you back to your parents,' he added, releasing her hands.

Thoughts swirled through Aliénor's head as the two of them walked side by side up the gentle slope to the château. There were two conclusions she could draw from the exchange with Ralf, she decided. Yes, the Smith — Peter — *had* once again become a thorn in the Germans' flesh. On the other hand, he was keeping his activities well away from her area. She didn't know whether to be elated by the news, or even more afraid.

10

A fitful breeze had sprung up, pushing rain clouds in from the south-west. Cycling along the long lane that led to Suzanne's farmhouse, Aliénor had to clutch at her straw hat to stop it flying off, and was glad of the wool jersey she'd knotted across her shoulders. How many times in the last two months had she made this journey? she asked herself, her spirits as sombre as the clouds. Even the rare measure of freedom she'd been granted the last few days failed to lighten her mood: her parents were spending five days with her father's younger sister — Aliénor's aunt, her cousin Joséphine's mother — who lived the other side of Poitiers. They had left four days before, travelling by horse-drawn taxi and train, and would be returning late the next day, Saturday.

The tall double gates were open, and Aliénor cycled in, her attention caught by young Jérôme. He was racing round the courtyard, arms outstretched like wings either side of him, making aeroplane noises. Getting down from her bicycle and propping it against the wall, she crossed to Suzanne, who stood in the open doorway of the kitchen, holding her baby against her shoulder, and kissed her.

'No school today?' she asked with a smile, but mildly surprised too. It was the tenth of September. The new term was less than two weeks old.

'No.' The baby made a sound, and Suzanne jigged her in her arms. 'He said he had a tummy ache. I think it's something to do with the baby. He doesn't want to feel pushed out.'

'I'm sure you're right,' Aliénor murmured as Jérôme came zooming towards her, screeching to a halt. 'Are you a bomber or a fighter?' she asked, smiling as she kissed him hello. For a brief, sweet instant she found she could forget everything and simply share in the child's boyish enthusiasm for his game.

'Neither,' he said, very serious. 'I'm a passenger plane. Come on board. Quickly.' And without waiting for a reply he stretched his arms out and sped off round the courtyard again.

Aliénor turned back to Suzanne. 'Any news?' she asked.

'They got back safely. First thing this morning.' She smiled happily. 'Christian says this is the last time.'

'The last time?' Aliénor smiled back. 'I bet you're relieved.' She knew *she* was. Already she was conscious of a sense of release as the constant tension of the last two months eased from her shoulders. 'It's — ' She slowed to a halt, unease stirring, raising the hackles along her neck. She glanced at Suzanne who was looking down at her baby, stroking her hair. 'The last time.' That was what Suzanne had said. The words echoed and re-echoed in Aliénor's brain. It was an odd turn of phrase.

Why should this be 'the last time'?

Her unease grew as she looked over at Jérôme, on the other side of the courtyard now, his aeroplane noises louder than ever. Wouldn't a boy pretend to be a bomber or a fighter rather than a passenger plane? A picture flashed into her mind, Peter holding her the day he had gathered those feathers, his hands round her waist, what he'd said that day, and it all clicked into place.

'Christian's been talking to Jérôme, hasn't he? About aeroplanes.' Her voice was sharp with anxiety, and she saw Suzanne's eyes widen in alarm.

'It's possible. They were chatting this morning.' Suzanne looked bewildered. She spoke rapidly, catching but not understanding Aliénor's anxiety. 'It's the first time Jérôme's played this aeroplane game.'

Aliénor hardly heard the confirmation of her fears. A hollow dread swooped through her and she swayed, faint with the shock of it.

'I must go,' she said, seized by a desperate urgency. Without even saying goodbye, she turned and ran across to her bicycle.

When? When would he leave? Would she be in time? She pedalled furiously but it was never fast enough. Her breath came in painful gasps. Would he leave during the day? Or would he wait until nightfall? So many questions, and she sobbed with frustration that she didn't have the answers.

Her hat blew off. No time to stop and retrieve it. No time to stand in the trees and see if all was safe at the hut. She cycled right up to it, let her bicycle drop to the ground, ran round to the back, pushed open the door.

Christian was there, by the mantelpiece, alarm in his face, his hand at his belt going for his knife. From the corner of her eye she saw his stance ease, his hand drop to his side. Her chest heaved as her gaze swept the room. Two makeshift beds, two chairs, pots, pans, tools hanging on the walls, no space for anything else. He wasn't there.

Her shoulders sagged. She'd come to the end of her tether. She couldn't go on any more. She'd arrived too late.

Christian reached past her to push the door to, and that was when she saw it, on the earth floor, hidden by the open door. His suitcase. It bulged slightly, and a length of string had been passed through the handle and round it to keep it shut if the catches failed. Relief washed over her. He hadn't left yet. But he was packed, ready to go.

'He's flying back to England, isn't he?' Her voice shook.

'Yes. Tonight. Shortly before midnight.'

Christian must have seen the misery — the defeat — in her face, for with a small sound he took her in his arms and held her to him. She made no protest. She so much wanted to be comforted. Peter used to stroke her hair like that, murmur soft words, just as Christian was doing now.

She pulled away from him, and wiped her eyes with the heel of her hand. 'Where is he?' she asked in a voice choked with emotion.

'He's saying goodbye.'

'I — I don't understand.'

'Here. I'll show you.' Christian opened the door, beckoning her to follow him. There was a new-found confidence about him, and it occurred to Aliénor he had gained immensely from the time spent with Peter. 'Over there,' he said, gesturing towards the forest.

Aliénor stared blankly. 'Where? I can't see him.' There was an edge of panic to her voice. And then she understood. 'You mean the path.' It was the path that led past her spring and on to the vantage point with the view over the château. The path that led to the spot where she'd told Peter there could be no future for the two of them.

With an uneasy smile she squeezed Christian's arm and set off towards the trees. She wasn't sure what she was hoping for, wasn't sure what she would find, knew only that she had to see him one more time.

★   ★   ★

It had begun to rain when she saw him. He was making his way back down the slope which led uphill to the vantage point. She saw him start when he caught sight of her. His face lit up, she was sure of it, and she thought for one joyous moment he was going to race towards her and sweep her into his arms. But he slowed his pace, and his smile as he came nearer was unreadable, the polite smile of a stranger. It was as if a spark had been extinguished.

He stopped about a metre away. 'You look well.' His tone was carefully neutral.

'I'm not. I've been sick with worry for you.' Her voice was unsteady. Tears were not far from the surface. 'You look — thin.' 'Gaunt' was the word. She was shocked. The colour he'd had when she'd seen him last was gone. His eyes were dark smudges in his pale face.

'I've been busy. No time to eat or sleep properly.'

'I know. I heard.' She couldn't take her eyes from his face. His beautiful face, despite its pallor and the hollows under his cheekbones. His beautiful hair too. He'd flattened it with water and combed it back from his forehead, but tufts of it stood up in the unruly spikes she loved so much. Instinctively she stepped forward a pace. Her eyes met his and there was wonder in her expression as she brushed her fingertips along the line of his jaw.

At first he didn't react. Then he leaned his cheek against her touch, and her heart stood still.

'Mélisande, my dearest.' He took her hand in his, pressed a kiss into her palm with lips that trembled. And all at once he was wrapping his arms round her waist, lifting her off her feet, hugging her to him, rocking her from side to side in a wild exhilarating embrace that set her pulses racing.

'Mélisande, my sweet Mélisande.' He'd buried his face in her hair, spoke in that gruff voice that touched her to the depths. 'I thought I'd never see you again. I thought you were lost to me forever.'

'I couldn't stop thinking about you,' she breathed as he set her down, his arms still tight around her, her body still rocking from side to side with his. Raindrops spattered on to her face, deflected by the leaves of the trees above them, mingling with the tears that were wet on her cheeks. Tears of pure happiness for she was in his arms again. 'Every time you went on an operation, I was so afraid.'

He stilled, lifting his head from her hair, his hands coming up to her shoulders. 'That's over now. No more operations.' He spoke gently, as though unwilling to hurt. 'I'm being flown out of here. Tonight.'

A raindrop — or a tear — slipped

down her cheek. 'I know. And I don't think I can bear it. I love you, Peter.'

The words hung in the air between them. They spoke simple truth. She wouldn't retract them.

'Oh Mélisande.' His voice was husky with emotion and he drew her into the length of his body, his hands low at her waist. There was a change in him now, a fresh impetus to what he did, a new intensity. 'You've no idea how I've dreamed of this moment.' His hands held her, pressing her hard against him. His kiss was long, insistent, increasingly urgent, and Aliénor gasped as an answering desire, fierce, equally urgent, uncurled deep inside her.

'Not here,' she whispered a long while later as his fingers went to the top button of her blouse.

'Where, then?'

'Come with me.'

His hand, work-roughened, clasped hers as she led him along the path before turning off to the right along a track so narrow they had to go in single file. She was heading for the spring. The rain had stopped but drops of water fell on them as they passed or were caught, bright and sparkling, by the sunlight that filtered through the trees. Again and again she turned to touch her fingers to his face, his hair, his shoulders, scarcely daring to believe he was there, with her. Again and again he caught her to him, murmuring her name, kissing her. Each time she looked into his eyes with breathless wonder, oblivious to the brambles that snagged at her clothes.

'Wait.' She'd seen honeysuckle, twisting up towards the light, the scent from its flowers fresh and vibrant in the newly-cleaned air. The stems were too tough to pick, and she watched Peter's long fingers as he cut through one with his knife. 'Two,' she said. 'We need two, one each.'

'My mysterious Mélisande,' he said, and her heart thudded as he kissed her again.

And soon they were at the spring

where fat bubbles welled, any sound the water made drowned in the soughing of the wind through the trees. Circles of sunlight spilled through the leaves and danced on the curtain of ivy that hung from the wall of rock on the far side before coiling into a bed on the woodland floor.

There was a fever in her movements, Peter's too, she could sense it, as they each let a stem of honeysuckle drop to the spring from fingers that shook with desire. Fever as he twined his fingers in hers and brought her round to where the thick ivy lay.

'I've never done this before,' she said, suddenly afraid, and he wrapped her in his arms, his hands moving from her back to the nape of her neck before tangling in her hair, drawing her head down to his shoulder.

'I know that, my dearest,' he said into her hair. 'You'll be safe with me.'

His words, his touch, were sweet caresses, so very tender, so very loving that her skin sang with the beauty of it.

She looked into his eyes, those eyes she loved so much.

'Kiss me,' she said. 'Hold me. Make love to me.' And she felt him, too, tremble as he drew her down to the soft bed of ivy.

★　★　★

She gave a little start and wondered if she'd fallen asleep again.

'Don't move,' Peter said softly. He lay on his side, very close. He was propped on one elbow, his hand supporting his head, while his free hand traced leisurely circles up and down her arm. 'I could look at you for ever.'

Something like a blush suffused his skin, and a smile curved his lips. She reached up and touched her fingers to his jaw, rough with the promise of the next day's beard, then to her own jawline, and thought that she too, probably, had that same rosy flush to her skin, the same wondering smile.

She let her arm drop back above her

head. The other lay across her stomach. She felt drowsy and languorous, loved and protected. 'Is it always like this? So — ' She paused, searching for the word. ' — exquisite?'

A teasing light came into his eyes. 'Well, I could boast . . . ' He left the remark trailing, and she gave a happy laugh and stretched her arms and legs and spine, feeling as sensuous as a cat rolling on its back, stretching out its limbs in the summer sun.

She looked beyond him, out to the woodland. The wind through the trees had died away, while the water bubbling up from the spring was the very faintest of murmurs. It was so peaceful here. But the air was darkening already, she saw, sleepy no more. The chill of the approaching autumn evening was on her skin, and she was seized by a different kind of urgency, the urgency of knowing their time together was running out.

'We must go.' It was as if he'd read her mind. There was a great sadness in his voice and in the gaze that moved over her features. He bent towards her and his lips took hers in a lingering kiss that sent whispers of pleasure across her skin. One last kiss in this special place, she thought. He drew away, stroked a caress, infinitely tender, along the line of her jaw and up into her hair.

'Oh Peter — '

Taking her hand, he stood up, bringing her up with him. 'Get dressed,' he said. 'We've got to go.' He was leaving at nightfall. His hands on her shoulders, he turned her round to where her clothes lay in an untidy heap.

She stared at them numbly. It couldn't end yet. She turned back to Peter, desire curling through her as her gaze swept over his beautiful body.

'I want to come with you to the airfield.'

Reaching down for his trousers, he straightened and looked at her. She saw his eyes move up and down her body, a mirror-action to her own. It was strange, she thought: normally self-conscious about her height and long, gangling limbs, she hadn't once felt shy at being naked in his presence.

'No,' he said. 'It's too dangerous. You'd be out after curfew for a start. And if a German patrol found you — ' He shook his head. 'I won't risk it.'

With a shiver she stooped to pick up her underwear. 'I'll be going with *you*. There's no risk. And Christian'll look after me on the way back.'

'No.' She saw him tug on his trousers, button up the fly. 'Besides, your parents will raise the alarm if you're not back by early evening.'

'No they won't. They're not there. They're visiting relatives. Only the servants are there.' He hesitated, and she pressed home her advantage. 'I want to spend every minute I can with you, Peter. Who knows when we'll see each other again?'

A look of pain crossed his face. He closed his eyes, opened them again. 'Yes,' he said. 'You're right. Come to the airfield with me. We must make the most of every moment.'

He crossed over to her and started buttoning her blouse. 'Listen, Mélisande, this is important.' He spoke low and fast as if urgency had caught him too in its mesh. 'If anything happens — ' He placed the flat of one hand against her stomach. ' — you know what I mean — or anything else — you're to get word to me. Tell Christian. His contact in Scévolles forest'll get a message through to London.'

'Yes.' She placed her hand over his at her stomach. 'Yes. I hadn't thought of that.' Surprisingly, perhaps, she wasn't worried by the possibility. She had complete faith in him, she realised.

'One day, God willing, this war will end. If the Allies win, and it looks as if it's starting to go their way, if they do the Germans will leave France, and I'll be free to come for you. But if I can't for some reason, you must come to me. Do you understand?'

'Yes. But — '

His hands came up to cup her face. 'Peter Maybury, The Manor House, Kingsbridge, Surrey.' He bent to touch a kiss to her lips. 'Repeat it, my dear.'

'Peter Maybury, The Manor House, Kingsbridge, Surrey,' she said, stumbling over the unfamiliar pronunciation.

He wrapped his arms round her, pulling her to him. 'We belong together, you and I. You can't marry Henri, you know that, don't you?'

Henri. She pulled away, conscious of a hollow sinking feeling. Henri couldn't have been further from her mind. She hadn't thought about him once all day. Her troubled eyes moved over the face of the man she loved. Much as she longed to agree with him, she knew things could never be that straightforward.

'I — Let's not think about that now,' she said, aware even as she spoke that she was storing up nothing but trouble for the future.

11

The moon was both a blessing and a curse. A waxing moon, it sent its light over hills and valleys, forests and fields, an eerie light that stole the colour from everything it touched, transforming the night into a world of monochrome shadows.

It had passed its zenith, and was in front of the three of them as they cycled west. The Milky Way was a gauzy veil above and behind them, trailing across the million bright sparks of light that gleamed against the dark velvet of the sky. Under other circumstances, Aliénor would have thought it a beautiful night. But tonight the moon, the stars, and the cloudless sky only made her shiver, and she was grateful for the jersey and trousers she wore.

'Moonlight's essential,' Peter had said shortly before they set off, after Aliénor had questioned the wisdom of travelling when the moon was so nearly full. 'The pilot needs it to help him make out the various landmarks.' He let go of her, his hand slipping from her waist just long enough to place his suitcase on the rack behind the saddle of his bicycle and loop a length of rope under and over to keep it in place. The bicycle had belonged to Suzanne's father. It was old and heavy and Peter intended leaving it at the airfield. 'If I were him, I'd look for where the river Vienne meets the Loire, follow the Loire west, and turn south when I saw the castle at Saumur.'

'And after that, all he's got to do,' Christian had added, pulling his beret down over his forehead, 'is find one tiny field in the middle of nowhere.'

It had been a moment of something approaching humour at the start of a journey that was stretching Aliénor's nerves close to breaking point. They'd cut through fields and skirted woods, keeping well away from towns and villages, a circuitous route to cover the fifteen kilometres between the grape-pickers' hut and the airfield.

The track they were now taking followed the top line of a ridge running parallel to the main road below. Night noises came to her through the cold air. Foxes barked, birds called out in alarm, owls screeched. Flying insects brushed against her. And all the while an urgent refrain beat in her ears: *so little time. So little time left.*

'Not far now.' Peter kept his voice down. She could hear the strain in it. A windmill loomed on their left. Beyond it, further away, she could see the spire of the church at Saint Léger, a dark shadow against the lighter shadow of the sky. No light was visible from the houses and shops grouped round the church. All windows and doors were shuttered.

'Stop.' His arm came out. She brought her bicycle to a halt and stood totally still. She could hear his breathing, Christian's too. Then she heard it, the rumble of a lorry engine coming closer. Only when she saw its dark outline go past along the road below did she let the tension ease from her shoulders.

They took the path on their right that sloped downhill, crossed the main road, and headed fast along the track edged by woodland that would take them to the airfield.

'Is that it?' 'Airfield' was a misnomer, Aliénor thought. Dismayed, she scanned the short strip of land before her, prickly with corn stubble, pale against the line of trees and hedges on the far side. It was just a field, and was surely far too small for a plane to land or take off safely.

'It'll do.' Peter had come to stand behind her. His face nuzzled against her cheek, her hair, his arms crisscrossing her chest, hands low on her hips, pulling her hard against him. She curled her hands round his arms and leaned back against him, loving the strength of his arms, the weight of his body against hers as he rocked her from side to side. A bittersweet embrace. Make the most of it, she told herself, for he would soon be gone.

'Here come the others,' he said into her hair. 'Nearer the time, they'll light torches to guide the plane in.' Releasing his hold, he squeezed her upper arms and stepped forward a pace, bringing her with him.

Four figures had detached themselves from the shadows, their clothes dark, their faces white ovals in the moonlight. Like Christian, they wore berets, the unofficial uniform of the Resistance.

'Ah, so this is the one . . . ' He was the oldest of the four, his voice cultured, and full of good humour and charm as he shook her hand. The pipe he held clamped between his teeth was unlit, as was the cigarette stuck to the lips of one of the others.

There were handshakes all round, claps on the back, and hugs, and Aliénor noted with pride the warmth and respect these men accorded Peter.

Warmth and respect for mild, unassuming Christian too.

'How long?' Peter asked.

'Half an hour.' It was the man with the pipe who spoke. 'We've got men on all the roads. Armed men. If nothing else, they'll fire warning shots if they see any Germans.'

Aliénor tugged at Peter's sleeve. 'Hold me.' Her voice was scarcely more than a whisper. And he pulled her into his embrace and into a kiss of such sweet intensity that her whole body ached with the beauty of it. She didn't know how long he held her in the circle of his arms, knew only that she could have stayed there forever.

All at once she stilled. Peter too. And Christian, who stood with the others some five metres away. They could all hear it, the faintest of sounds, far away, like the drone of a bumblebee.

Suddenly all was movement. The four men took off, running across the field in four different directions, pulling flint-boxes and dry wadding from their pockets as they went. And Christian was running towards her and Peter, holding the suitcase out.

Peter took it, set it down, pulled Christian into a quick, fierce hug. 'Look after her for me.' His voice was gruff. 'See her home safe. She means the world to me.'

'I know.' Christian's eyes, like Peter's, glittered in the moonlight. 'I will.'

Peter turned to her, and she flew into his arms, clinging to him, as if she'd never let him go.

'I have to go now, my dearest.' He pressed a hard kiss to her mouth. 'I'll be back. You know that, don't you?'

The noise was much louder now, close overhead, a mechanical sound like the motor of a car.

'No.' She couldn't bear it. But even as she spoke, her hands released their hold. She had to let him go, she knew it. 'I love you so much.'

She looked across at the field, and panic shot through her. The aeroplane had landed already. A figure slid down the ladder fixed to the outside and started running towards the nearest torch-holder. A matt black shadow against the paler corn stubble, the plane was taxiing round, ready for take-off. *No time. No time left.* With one last kiss on her lips, Peter had picked up his suitcase and was running, long legs taking him fast across the field. She saw him scramble up the ladder. He paused and turned — despite the fickle play of light and dark, she was sure of it — and looked back at her before climbing into the cockpit behind the pilot, and her heart stood still for that instant.

She watched mutely as the plane moved down the field, slowly at first, rapidly gaining speed; wasn't even sure of the exact moment it rose from French soil, taking her Peter with it, back to England. *Back to England.* There was a finality in the words that was more than she could stand. She turned away, slamming her hand to her mouth. And the tears came; long wretched sobs drawn from the very depths of her soul.

★   ★   ★

'Mélisande, come on, we've got to go.' There was urgency in Christian's voice. He'd put his arm across her shoulders, and now drew her with him towards their bicycles.

As she started to pedal, she looked back. She'd thought it couldn't get any worse, but it could. Peter's bicycle lay there, on the ground, forlorn. Would it be left there to rust? Or would the new arrival make use of it?

She was numb, dazed. Her brain refused to operate. She followed Christian blindly, without question, along the track which would take them over the main road and up to the windmill. It was darker here, the moon hidden by the trees, and the going was slower.

They hadn't yet reached the cross-roads when Christian glanced back at her. 'Listen. Can you hear it? Come on.' His voice was low and harsh.

She stared at him blankly. It came from some distance away: a dry sound, repeated over and over, like fireworks, or twigs on a bonfire snapping. Aliénor couldn't place it at first. And then she understood. Rifle fire. Instinctively she started pedalling faster, and saw Christian was doing the same. It had to be one of the groups of men placed on roads near the airfield. Were they attacking a German patrol? Or warning the men at the airfield that Germans were nearby? Either way, it meant trouble.

She pedalled furiously, keeping close to Christian, aware of another sound much nearer, much louder. The rumble of a heavy motor. Her first thought was that the aeroplane, and Peter, had come back. But her hope was short-lived. The noise came from ground level and meant danger, not joy.

'Get into the woods. Quick.' Christian's voice, the words an urgent rasp.

They were only metres from the crossroads.

It was an army lorry, a dark mass, going at speed along the main road. The driver must have caught the movement, or perhaps the glint of metal, as she and Christian scrambled down from their bicycles. It skidded to a halt, brakes squealing, reversed, and came forward again, turning into the track they were on. Two rectangles of feeble light came from its masked headlights, failing utterly to pierce the darkness.

The lorry slowed but didn't stop. Sound filled the air: the staccato shouts of men, the crack of tyres on stone, the thud as booted feet hit the ground. Two men, dark shadows in the darkness, jumped down from the back. Each carried a rifle.

It had been the work of a moment. Aliénor stood as if paralysed. Christian too, she saw. Then, 'Move!' he hissed. But she couldn't. From further down the track came the rat-a-tat-a-tat of machine gun fire. The lorry had clearly arrived at the airfield. The aeroplane had long gone. Peter was safe. But what of the four Frenchmen? And the newcomer? She saw the swift-moving shadow as the butt of a rifle swooped through the air towards Christian and heard the dull thwack as it made contact with flesh; his cry as he went down.

With a cry of her own, she spun round and started to run. Too late. The second man was on her before she'd taken two strides, booted foot tangling with her legs, lifting her feet off the ground. The air was shocked from her lungs as she fell through spikes of broom and crashed to the ground.

She must have passed out. Just for a second or two. Or had it been longer? She didn't know. She didn't have the strength to move; could only heave breath into her raw lungs. She lay sprawled, not quite flat on her face, on ground that was still damp from the afternoon's rain. The rich peaty smell of the soil was all around. Pieces of twig dug into one cheek and the palms of her hands.

'Hey, this one's a woman.' It was a voice that had broken only a year or two before, speaking German of course. Aliénor froze.

'Bring her over.' The voice of an older man, a few metres away. She heard a grunt, the sounds of something bulky being shifted, a muffled groan from Christian.

Nausea rose. What had the soldier done to him? Instinct took over and she braced herself, hands moving down to protect her stomach, and was partially ready when a boot thumped into her hipbone, kicking her over on to her back, sending spears of pain lancing through her.

'Get up, bitch.' She didn't understand all the words, but the tone was unmistakable.

Hands seized her wrists, yanking her to her feet. She had to fight to keep her balance, desperate not to be thrown against the man. She could smell his sweat and stale tobacco. Fear pounded through her, and there was a roaring in her ears. She jerked her wrists from his grip, but found them seized again. She was turned round, her hands wrenched up behind her back, as high as her shoulder blades.

'Bitch,' she heard again as she cried out. He held both her hands in one of his, and had twisted her hair round the other, dragging her head back. Now he kneed her in the back, propelling her forward.

She heard a metal door open and clang shut, and boots move across the ground; then saw two long thin rectangles of light like narrowed robot's eyes and realised the roaring she could hear was the engine of the lorry back from the airfield.

'They got away.' The newcomer spoke with authority. An officer, clearly. His anger was palpable. Aliénor didn't understand it all, but enough to cause a ripple of glee to bring a grim smile to her face. One more defeat, albeit minor, for the Germans. 'Here, handcuff them,' the officer said, 'and get them into the lorry.'

The soldier let go of her hair, snapped circles of cold metal round her wrists, and bundled her towards the lorry. She was pushed up and over the tail-gate, and tumbled sprawling onto the slats inside. It was dark beneath the canvas, but she sensed the presence of many men. She could smell their sweat, the leather of boots and belts, and hot gun oil. Her heart was thumping in a queasy, shallow beat. She'd never been so scared in all her life. Frantically she started to struggle to her feet, trying not to sob with frustration because her hands were fastened behind her back. She heard grunts of exertion and a groan from Christian as he too was pushed into the lorry, knocking her back down again as he landed in a heavy heap across her legs.

'Sit them up.' It was the officer, standing outside, speaking through the gap in the canvas. He shone a torch into her face. Aliénor twisted her head away and saw eight men watching her with interest, four each side, sitting on benches and holding rifles, other weapons and equipment down the middle between them.

'A woman. Christ,' the officer said. 'Hands off, do you hear?'

The men all spoke at once, greeting the order with jeers and, by the sound of it, ribald comments. But there was respect for the officer's authority, she thought, and she hoped they would obey him. She felt nauseous, and only too aware of the additional hazard that a man, surely, would never have to face.

12

She and Christian were hauled into a sitting position side by side on the floor of the lorry, their two assailants jumped in, and the lorry moved off.

She was afraid, so very afraid. Her brain was frozen, incapable of thought. The hip the soldier had kicked still throbbed, and muscles were torn, she was sure of it, at her shoulders. She wasn't thirsty. She'd drunk water from the spring. How long ago it seemed, now. But she'd had nothing to eat since breakfast at least sixteen hours before. And at some point soon, a more urgent need would make itself felt.

When Christian moved and murmured a very quiet 'Okay?', her relief that he was still alive, still able to speak, was immense. But retaliation was immediate. A rifle butt thudded into some part of him, the force of the blow sending his body into hers. She heard his 'oof' of pain and shock, and a snarled 'Shut up' from one of the soldiers. She closed her eyes against the sounds and leant her head against Christian's. She needed that reassuring contact with a friend, and sensed he did too. It had been a swift, brutal lesson: they must say or do nothing to antagonise these men.

Her brain began to function again, though the fear was still there, a constant shadow that made her circumspect. When the lorry turned a corner or jolted over the rails of a level crossing, she was thrown against the legs of one or other of the soldiers. Pushing her back into a sitting position invariably involved groping her breasts, and catcalls and jeers from the others. Her cheeks burned with shame, but she said nothing, forcing herself to endure the humiliation, knowing that anything she might say would provoke an immediate, violent reaction.

She didn't know where the lorry was

taking them, and her mind shrank from thinking about what awaited the two of them at their destination. Would her father be able to get her out of this mess? she wondered. Her and Christian. Surely he'd be able to pull a few strings with General Hartmann to secure their release. Even as the faint flicker of hope buoyed her spirits, another thought came to deflate them. Her parents were away. They wouldn't be back till much later in the day. There were hours to endure before then.

She heard the driver change down a gear as the lorry rumbled over cobbles up a long slope. They were in a town. Apprehension swirled in her stomach. This was it.

The lorry stopped. She heard voices, feet on paving stones, the opening and closing of the lorry's passenger side door. The canvas flaps behind her were tied back, and the officer shone his torch on two of his men.

'You, and you, stay here. Make sure these two don't move a muscle. Rest of you, back to barracks.'

As all but two of the soldiers picked up their gear, strode past her and jumped down to the ground, Aliénor twisting round to look out of the lorry. The moon, close to setting, cast a meagre light, but it was enough to see the façade of a large building, tall arched windows, and the Nazi swastika draped over the front; and her heart quickened as she saw where she was. Loudun town hall. So near home, and yet so far. She'd never see her home again, she was sure of it. Again she felt that sickening lurch as hope flared, only to die the very next second.

More footsteps, and the figure of a tall man came out of the shadows to join the officer. 'Finished for the night, Major?'

Aliénor barely heard the other man's ''Fraid not, Captain. I've got to take these two down to Poitiers.' Ralf! She recognised the voice first, and saw his face, pale in the darkness. She must have made a noise, for he turned to look at her. 'Aliénor!'

'Do you know her?' It was the major.

'Aliénor Rochefontaine de Montfort. Her parents own a lot of land south-west of here.' He spoke hurriedly, his eyes on her.

The other officer whistled. 'She'd have done better to stay at home stitching tapestries.'

'Why? What's she done? What's she doing here?'

'We found the two of them — ' He shone the torch on Christian ' — less than five hundred metres from a field where a plane had just landed and taken off. Draw your own conclusions.'

Ralf flinched as though he'd been punched. Had his thoughts flashed back to the last time they'd spoken, when she'd asked him about the Smith? She saw him swallow and square his shoulders. 'There's been some mistake. You've got to let her go.'

'I can't do that. She and her pal are as guilty as hell. Besides, I've already radioed ahead. They're expecting them.'

'I know her. She's not involved. She can't be. You're making a mistake.'

The major's expression hardened and he reached up to untie the canvas flaps. 'In that case, she'll be found innocent and sent back here, won't she, Captain?' He laid a slight extra emphasis on his final word, to remind Ralf no doubt that he was outranked.

Aliénor saw Ralf stiffen as he turned away, his face tight with anger, before the canvas came down and she and Christian were in darkness again.

'So where are you taking them?' There was a disquieting edge to his voice, as though he knew what the answer was, an answer his mind recoiled from.

'Where do you think? Pierre Levée prison, of course.'

Aliénor heard Christian's sharp intake of breath and a muttered 'Best place for them' from one of the soldiers left to guard them. Fear washed over her. It was the worst possible news. Run entirely by the

Germans and dealing with threats to the security of Occupied France, the Pierre Levée was notorious for the brutality of its interrogations and its use of torture. Few walked out free. For most of those who were brought through its doors, the future held the prospect of deportation or death by firing squad. Aliénor heard Ralf's clipped, angry footfall grow ever more distant. Leaning her head against Christian's shoulder, she gulped back a shaky sob as fear shuddered through her and the last flicker of hope was extinguished.

* * *

Even in the small hours of the night, the noise never stopped: the scrabble of little creatures across the concrete floor of her cell, the clang of feet on the metal staircase outside her door, from a neighbouring cell the low inhuman moans of a body in pain, and, shamefully, the angry responses from fellow prisoners nearby. Aliénor had clapped her hands over her ears and rocked herself from side to side. She couldn't soothe the hurt of the person who suffered. She couldn't offer herself any shred of hope. She could do nothing. She was powerless.

The cell smelt of must. The walls were cold and clammy to the touch. She had a metal bench just long enough for her to lie on — although she'd remained sitting — and, thankfully, a bucket. There was no food, no water, no light. She was alone. The last time she'd seen Christian, he was being taken up the stairs to the first or second floor. She'd seen apprehension in his eyes, masked by the thick lenses of his glasses, and knew it was reflected in hers.

Now, as the first glimmers of dawn started to chase the shadows away, there were more voices, heavy doors slamming, shouts, howls of pain and protest, a cacophony of sound, and Aliénor felt as if her nerves were being ripped ragged.

Fear came again, renewed fear, wave after wave of it, rolling over her skin, round and round. It would be her turn soon. She wanted to be brave. How she hoped she'd be brave! She paced the cell, her bunched fists punching down in unison, willing strength into mind and body. What did she know? What could she tell them? Christian's real name, that was all. She knew nothing of his contacts in Scévolles forest. It had been kept that way deliberately.

Oh God. She sank down on to the bench, legs all at once too weak to take her weight. She knew Peter's full name and address. It was information about the Smith that they'd dearly love to have. What if they tortured it out of her? How soon before she told them all she knew about the man she loved? She stood up again, fast, and retched emptily into the bucket just as the door to her cell burst open.

It was a man wearing civilian clothes. He scarcely looked at her, but simply swivelled her round, cuffed her hands behind her, and prodded her out of the cell and along a long corridor, all with a low-level violence that was all the more shocking for its casualness. Her footsteps echoed, prisoners called out, there were cries, shouted orders. Aliénor's nerves jangled. Her bruised hip throbbed more than ever. She needed to use the bucket again. How would she ever survive this?

'You're going in here.' Her guard seized her wrists, bringing her to a halt, and rapped on a door.

'Come in.'

The guard opened the door and pushed her through with such force that she almost lost her balance. She had the impression of a large room, its walls painted cream, and saw a table bare but for a phone, an ashtray, and one of the tall peaked caps worn by high-ranking officers. There was a plain wooden chair this side of the table, a leather-covered office chair the other. But her attention was caught and held by the figure who stood with his back to her, hands clasped behind him, looking out of the window. He wore the grey uniform of the Gestapo. Her heart gave a single, painful thump: her interrogator.

He turned round and her eyes widened in shock. 'You!'

'Take the cuffs off,' he said to the guard, and when the man had done so, 'You can go.' He moved a pace or two away from the window. The limp had gone, she saw. 'Sit down.'

She sat. She was trembling, more afraid than ever. She glanced down at her hands on her lap, then looked up again, drawn to the scar that slashed across his face. She swallowed, willing her voice not to shake. 'Colonel Ostermeyer.'

He came and leant, half sitting, against the side of the table, an intimidating presence, so close that she could smell his tobacco and the soap he used. She looked down at her hands again. Perhaps, that way, she'd give less away.

Long seconds stretched into minutes.

'So, what have we got?' He spoke as if he were engaged in nothing more than a pleasant chat. 'You, the daughter of Vincent and Thérèse Rochefontaine de Montfort. And Patrice Lebel, twenty-two, would-be teacher, on the run from the compulsory work programme.'

Alarm darted through her. She forced herself not to react. Had he interrogated Christian already? Was that how he knew so much about him?

'You were found just before midnight. Technically you weren't breaking the curfew, but we both know you would never have been able to get home in time. Correct?'

She looked up but said nothing. Her blood was pounding in her ears.

'So I'm here to ask you what you were doing less than five hundred metres from a field where a Lysander landed only minutes before. Did the plane drop an agent? Pick one up? Both?' His tone was persuasive, inviting her to confess all. Aliénor sucked in a long shuddering breath, expelling it immediately, too racked with tension to hold oxygen in her lungs.

He came away from the table and straightened. 'You of course, courageous Resistance fighter that you are, will say nothing.' Her eyes grew wide and wary, her hackles standing on end, as he moved round behind her; but she wouldn't — couldn't — look round. 'As you can see, I know a lot already. It wouldn't take much to find out the rest.' She could only sit there, incapable of movement, rigid with shock, when he picked up her hair, drawing the long thick mass over his hands. 'So I send you to my colleagues down in the cellars, some of whom have special techniques they reserve for their women . . . guests.'

The words hung in the air between them as he let her hair fall, then picked it up again, twisting his fingers in it. Her scalp was crawling; it was almost impossible to breathe.

His hands fell to her shoulders and

he began to massage the taut muscles there, his movements firm and sensuous, with a seductive quality that both sickened her and made her aware just how vulnerable she was in so many ways.

His fingers stilled, and for an instant there was no movement, no sound anywhere, as if the world stood poised, waiting.

'Frightened, Aliénor?'

The clang of boots on metal stairs pierced the silence, the slamming of a door, a man's cry of pain. Christian? Christian lying broken in a cell somewhere?

'You know I am.' Her mouth was so dry she could hardly speak. 'I'd be a fool not to be.'

'An effective deterrent then, perhaps.'

She kept silent, more wary than ever. If only she could see his face. But he stood behind her still, thumbs kneading lazy circles each side in the crook where her neck met her shoulders.

'I can get you out of here just this

once, Aliénor. There won't be a second time. Not even I have that much influence.'

She shook her head, not understanding. She couldn't see the connection with what had gone before. Get her out of here? What was this? Another weapon in his armoury? His hands lifted from her shoulders, and she heard the click of his boots on the lino-covered floor as he came round to lean against the table again. She heard him light a cigarette, and smelt the smoke he exhaled. But she kept her gaze fixed on her own hands, stock-still in her lap, as if they were the one sure point in a world of hideous danger.

'You're free to go,' he said. 'My driver will take you home.'

She did look up then, guarded eyes meeting his. There was no softness in his face; he wasn't smiling. His expression was unreadable. She ran her tongue round her mouth. 'I — I don't understand.'

'Captain Horelbeck had a busy night.

He phoned General Hartmann, and your parents. When that led nowhere, he phoned me in Paris. Only I could get you out of this mess, he said. So I drove down and spoke to the head of the *Sicherheitsdienst* here who agreed with me that you were nothing more than an innocent bystander.'

Ralf? Was it possible? Aliénor was having difficulty taking it all in. Ralf had done all that for her?

'What about — Patrice?' She stumbled over the word. It was difficult to think of Christian by other than his code-name.

'You were together, so logically he's innocent too. But he's guilty of evading the compulsory work programme. He won't face a firing squad, but he'll be sent to the internment camp at Compiègne-Royallieu and on to work in Germany somewhere.'

A great surge of hope welled inside her. It was all beginning to sink in. It wasn't a trap. It was all true. Christian wasn't out of danger yet, not by a long chalk. But he had a chance. Now he faced what thousands of other young able-bodied Frenchmen faced, back-breaking poorly paid work in a factory or fields far from home. It wasn't good, but it could have been worse, much worse.

'But why?' she asked. 'Driving down through the night. Speaking to — Why should *you* do all that for *me*?'

He didn't answer straight away, taking smoke down deep into his lungs, expelling it in a long stream through his mouth. 'For the same reason as young Horelbeck, I imagine,' he said at last. There was anger in his movements as he stubbed his cigarette out. 'Stand up.'

He stood too, and all at once he was shockingly close to her. She tried not to look at the ugly scar that cut across his face. Before she could step back, he took her hands in his. His eyes, cold and searching, met hers. 'So when is your wedding to Henri d'Eparnelle? The twenty-fourth of December of next year, I believe.' His tone was conversational. It didn't surprise her that he knew the exact date — he knew a lot of things about a lot of people, she was sure — but her eyes were troubled as she gave a cautious nod. He released one of her hands, his fingers coming up to smooth strands of her hair back from her face. His hand moved on, behind her head, drawing her to him, and his mouth came down on hers.

Aliénor didn't know why she responded as she did. Perhaps it was the natural culmination after twenty-four hours that had stretched her emotions to the limits, from the highest peaks of exquisite joy to the deepest chasms of fear. Or perhaps she was dazed through lack of sleep and food. Or was it simply gratitude to Ernst Ostermeyer? He had almost certainly saved her life, after all. Whatever it was, she found herself closing her eyes, swaying forward, melting into the sweet intensity of his kiss. As his arms came round her, she was back in Peter's arms, greedy for his touch, and it was bliss.

Almost immediately, a matter of seconds, she came to her senses, and pulled away from him, chest heaving, her cheeks burning with shame.

He was close still, but didn't attempt to touch her. His mouth sketched a brief, cruel smile. 'Remember me on your wedding night.'

She saw some indefinable emotion narrow his eyes and tug at the corners of his mouth. It was a glimpse, gone in an instant, of a different, more vulnerable man.

'I could have made you happy,' he said, and there was regret in his smile now. He turned back to the table, adding, so quietly she almost didn't catch the words, '*He* won't.'

13

Aliénor knew almost immediately. A tautness in her breasts and a faint nausea at the smell of ersatz coffee told her, even before she missed her period. Surprisingly perhaps, she wasn't apprehensive, not then. Instead, she carried the knowledge around with her, a precious secret, not to be shared for the time being. Her parents had confined her to the château and its grounds but she didn't mind, one part of her marvelling at the instinct that made her want to stay at home and build a nest.

Her father had summoned her to his study the moment Colonel Ostermeyer's driver brought her back to the château. He stood on the far side of his desk, his back to her, looking out of the windows. Her mother wasn't there, and Aliénor didn't know whether to be relieved or worried by her absence. He didn't look round as Aliénor came in, closing the door behind her and coming to a halt in front of the desk. She was unwashed, her hair uncombed, and wearing the clothes she'd worn since breakfast the previous day. Physically she was safe: she'd been given bread and jam to eat, and a mug of water to drink, and she'd managed to seize an hour's fitful sleep on the journey. But mentally she was reeling still, her mind reliving over and over the horror of the last few hours.

The honeyed scent of wood from the log fire mingled with the hint of must from the books that lined most of the available wall space. There were gaps along the shelves, of course. As with his wines and paintings, her father had had the rarest, most valuable ones hidden behind a wall in the cellars, hastily put up in May 1940 as the German army and air force poured into France.

'Colonel Ostermeyer has been on the phone to me. Your mother and I had only just arrived home.' His tone was neutral. Aliénor supposed he was angry with her, but even if she could see his expression, she had no way of knowing. With rare exceptions, he hid his feelings behind a mask of bland good manners. 'He says he won't be able to get you out of trouble a second time.' He paused. 'It was good of him to do so this time, of course. But I dare say he had his reasons.' He turned to look at her, eyes sharp as they searched his daughter's features.

Aliénor flushed. 'He behaved — correctly, *père*.' *She* had been the wanton one, she thought, wretched and shocked still.

His mouth tightened. 'Your face tells a different story.' He came away from the window, crossing the room until he stood facing her across the desk. 'He says you've been working with the Resistance; that you were helping smuggle an enemy agent in or out of France last night. You don't deny it, I suppose.'

Her chin tilted. 'No.'

She watched uncertainly as he came round the desk, almost flinching when he took both her hands in his. Like her mother, he didn't welcome physical contact, and scarcely ever sought it.

'I'm proud of you, *ma fille*. Very proud.' Aliénor swallowed hard. Somehow, it was the last thing she'd expected to hear. 'But it must stop. You'll be risking yourself, your family, and your home if you continue. There must be no more of it.' He gave her hands a squeeze. 'Do you understand?'

'Yes. Yes I do.' Her voice was small and gruff. 'I promise, *père*.'

'You may go.' His hands dropped from hers and she turned to the door.

Later that same day, Aliénor pulled a cardigan on, buttoning it up against the early-evening chill. She'd washed, slept an uneasy sleep, and dressed in clean clothes. Now renewed urgency gripped her. She had to speak to Ralf.

She saw him on the lawn near the terrace, trailing behind General Hartmann and Major Kellner as the three of them headed away from her towards the north wing. The terrace was empty apart from a maid clearing glasses. There was no sign of her parents.

'Ralf,' she called after him.

He turned, and there was no mistaking the relief and happiness in the smile that lit his face. The other two soldiers, deep in conversation, carried on walking. They probably hadn't even heard her. Ralf came towards her, almost at a run, pulling his cap off. He looked as if he wanted to sweep her up into his arms, but caught himself just in time.

'*Mademoiselle*.' He stopped a metre away and stood with his cap in his hand, arms stiffly at his side, very straight, very correct. 'I was hoping I might see you.'

'Oh Ralf.' Without thinking, she stretched up, her lips touching his cheek in a light kiss. His skin was cool, and rough with the next day's beard. 'It's so good to see you.' She spoke with genuine pleasure, the sense of urgency that had propelled her to seek him out momentarily forgotten. 'I can never thank you enough. I don't know what would have happened if you hadn't phoned Colonel Ostermeyer.'

His expression hardened. 'Believe me, if I'd had any alternative, I wouldn't have done.'

Aliénor shivered as her mind went back to the hours she'd spent at the Pierre Levée prison. 'He used shock tactics to deter me from — uh — any further involvement.'

It was a tacit admission of guilt, and she saw Ralf's eyes narrow. But all he said was, 'He did nothing — untoward?' As if at some unspoken signal, they started walking slowly, side by side, away from the château.

Aliénor's gaze went to the trees fifty metres or so to her left. He'd had a limp; had needed a stick the afternoon she'd walked with him through those trees. Her scalp tingled as she recalled the way his fingers had tangled in her hair. Even now. She shook her head, unwilling to lie to Ralf, distressed by the effect that man had had on her.

They walked on in silence for a while.

'Will his tactics work?'

She turned and looked at him. 'Yes. I promised my father.' The cawing of rooks returning to their treetop roosts for the night reached her through the September air. 'Ralf,' she went on, 'I need to know what's happened to Patrice Lebel. Can you find out for me? Please.' She sensed him stiffen beside her, his expression unreadable, and she hesitated before plunging on. She'd all but confessed her guilt minutes before. She surely had nothing to lose. 'The aeroplane. Can you find out if anything happened to it?'

He gave a low whistle between his teeth. 'You don't ask much.'

She touched his sleeve, bringing him to a halt. 'Please, Ralf.'

He faced her. All at once his blue eyes were as cold as Ernst Ostermeyer's. Aliénor met his gaze, willing him to agree to her request. He was her only hope.

'I can't promise anything. But I'll see what I can do.' He put his cap back on his head. 'At your service, *mademoiselle*,' he said, standing straight and clicking his heels together. He turned smartly and walked rapidly away towards the north wing.

Aliénor stood where she was and watched him go. The thought came unbidden that if she had a brother, she'd want him to be like Ralf.

★   ★   ★

With a sigh, Aliénor sank heavily on to the wooden bench seat and stared out across the lake. It was a beautiful afternoon in the last days of September. White clouds were reflected in the water, still apart from the occasional circle that spread slowly out as a fish or some other creature came up from below, only to dip down again unseen. The branches of the trees close by barely stirred in the breeze. Her lips curved into a sad smile. It was so peaceful here. The revving of a lorry and the shouts of soldiers that reached her could well belong to another world, far away.

It was just over two weeks before when she'd asked Ralf to help her, and she hadn't seen him since. The constant gnawing ache, a queasy mix of worry and lack of news that kept her awake each night, hadn't lessened. Her mind was numb, incapable of thought or feeling, as if her brain had closed down, blotting out not only the twelve nightmare hours that had begun bare minutes after the Lysander had taken off, but also the fear she felt for Christian and Peter. Had Colonel Ostermeyer kept his promise and sent Christian to a work camp in Germany? And Peter, her dearest Peter, had his plane taken him safely back to England? Would she ever see him again, know his touch, hear words of love from his lips, or was he lost to her forever? Tears, never far from the surface now, ran down her cheeks and she pressed her hand to her forehead, unable to stop the sobs that once again ripped through her.

A loud sound close by jolted her out of it. She twisted round on the bench, nerves on edge, eyes darting to the nearest tree. It was a pigeon, its wings flapping against the foliage as it scrambled clumsily into the inner branches. Aliénor let her shoulders relax, her hand going to her pocket for her handkerchief.

She blew her nose just as movement caught her eye. A man in the hated field-grey uniform was coming across the grass towards her. Her spirits brightened as she recognised him. It was Ralf. Did he have news for her? Good news?

She stood but forced herself to stay where she was. She needed the time to compose herself. Even so, his look when he drew near was one of concern mixed with something less easy to define, and she knew her eyes must be red-rimmed, her face blotchy from crying.

'Ralf, I'm so pleased to see you,' she said, smiling as she reached up to kiss him. 'Please sit down,' she went on, doing so herself and turning to face him.

He didn't return her smile. 'I've brought you news.' He sat, leaning forward, elbows resting on his knees. He'd taken his cap off and was turning it over and over between his two hands. 'It's not bad news.'

'Yes?'

'Lebel was sent to Compiègne-Royallieu, and on to a town called Wolfenbüttel. It's in the middle of Germany, fairly near Hanover. He's gone to the work camp there, not the prison.'

Aliénor breathed a sigh of relief. So Colonel Ostermeyer had kept his promise. She was grateful to him for that. Ralf's demeanour and his odd turn of phrase had made her uneasy, but his choice of words was surely the correct one. A work camp in Germany wasn't good news, but it was perhaps the best that could be hoped for in the circumstances.

Ralf shifted a fraction on the bench, and all at once Aliénor became aware he hadn't looked her in the eye all the time he'd been sitting, all his attention focused on the cap he moved between his hands.

Cold whispers of apprehension sped down her spine. 'Tell me.'

Still he couldn't look her in the eyes. 'Lebel fell and broke his arm.'

Something about his manner and the way he spoke told her the truth behind his statement. 'He didn't fall, did he?' Poor Christian. 'Was it — Colonel Ostermeyer?'

'No. He was on his way back to Paris when it happened.'

She fell silent, Ralf too, each deep in their own thoughts. It didn't escape her notice that he must have asked the same question she'd just put to him.

How would mild, studious Christian cope in a work camp far from home? Aliénor wondered, anger vying with concern. Would there even be a doctor or nurse to tend to his arm?

'*Scheiße!*' Ralf stooped, picked up a stone, and sent it skimming viciously across the water. 'We're not all thugs and bullies,' he growled, watching the fast-moving ripples the stone had caused.

Aliénor put her hand over his. 'Not all,' she agreed quietly.

'No planes were brought down over this area that night.' Ralf was looking at her hand. She hadn't moved it away. 'Something might have happened nearer the coast or over the Channel, it's impossible to say.' He turned to face her. 'There was someone on that aeroplane, wasn't there? Someone special.'

Not waiting for an answer, Ralf stood up with something close to anger in his movements, and her hand slid away from his. With a formal 'Don't stay out much longer, *mademoiselle*. Evening is coming,' he clicked his heels together, turned, and walked away.

'Yes,' Aliénor said simply, in answer to his question even though he'd gone. Peter was safe. Or at least he'd come through the first part of the journey. She had to believe he'd survived the rest. A smile softened the corners of her mouth as she placed her palms one on top of the other flat across her stomach.

★ ★ ★

'*Salope!* Slut!'

Aliénor cried out in shock as her mother slapped her a stinging blow across the cheek. She staggered back, fighting to keep her balance. It had had to come out of course. She couldn't keep it a secret forever. And she shouldn't have been surprised at her mother's vehemence.

By a strange twist of fate, it was Henri's mother, Hortense, who first noticed that her body was changing. She and Henri's father Auguste had come down to the château to spend the Christmas weekend with Aliénor and her parents. To her relief, work had kept Henri in Paris. It meant she could put off for a while longer the inevitable unpleasantness when she told him their marriage couldn't go ahead. He was hardly a passionate suitor. Her change of heart might hurt his pride, but no more than that, surely?

It was Christmas Day, and the five of them sat around the table in the small dining room, having a light lunch after the traditional feast, no feast at all by pre-war standards, the evening before.

'I must say, Aliénor,' Hortense said, taking a sip of her vegetable soup, 'when we last saw you, in November, you were looking very peaky.' Following tradition, she and her husband had come down to put flowers on her parents' grave in Poitiers on the first of November, All Saints' Day. Again, Henri had been tied up in Paris and hadn't come with them. 'But now,' she went on, 'you're positively blooming. I noticed it last night in the candlelight. You've filled out round the chin. Don't you agree, Thérèse?'

The silence lasted less than an instant. The two men were talking hunting and noticed nothing. Thérèse stilled, soup spoon poised in mid-air as her gaze flicked over her daughter's face. She smiled. 'Good country air, my dear Hortense. That's the secret.'

But Aliénor had seen the slight narrowing of her eyes and knew it wasn't the end of the matter.

The summons came as they finished dessert.

'Vincent, why don't you take our guests round the grounds? It's a perfect day for a walk.' It was a crisp, clear winter's afternoon. 'If you will excuse me, I have one or two more presents to wrap. Aliénor will help me.'

She stood now near one of the windows in her mother's bedroom, breathless with shock at the slap her mother had delivered, hands clenching as she faced her. It was an opulent room. Panels of cream and gold silk lined the walls while richly embroidered purple draperies hung round the bed and at the two pairs of windows. Aliénor's eye was caught by the bright emerald green of Hortense's coat and matching hat. She and the two men were about halfway down the tree-lined avenue which led to the gatehouse, well out of earshot.

'I am not a slut.' She was close to tears. But her voice was hard and she spaced the words in her anger, cut to the quick by the unfairness of the accusation.

It was as if her mother hadn't heard her. 'A slut carrying a German bastard.'

'No!' Shock jolted the denial from her. 'My baby's fa — '

'I'm not interested,' Thérèse cut in. 'Be quiet. Let me think.' She turned abruptly, then started pacing between the window and the bed. In a woman normally so controlled, her anger was frightening.

'My baby will not be a bastard. I am

going to marry the baby's father.'

Thérèse spun round, fury on her face. 'You are not. You are marrying Henri d'Eparnelle.'

'No. I don't love him,' Aliénor protested. 'And he doesn't love — '

'Love.' Her mother's scorn lashed at her like wind-driven rain. 'What has love got to do with it?' Her eyes narrowed, cold and implacable as they moved from her daughter's face to her stomach. 'Nothing must stop your marriage to Henri d'Eparnelle.'

'Look.' All at once Thérèse moved past her to the window. Her father and his two guests had reached the gatehouse and were turning back. 'You see these hangings?' Thérèse said. Her voice was low and fierce, her body taut with anger. She took a piece of the rich purple fabric between her two hands, then moved her hands apart, and the cloth simply split, a vertical split more than a metre long. A wispy cloud of fine purple dust puffed into the air along its length. 'They're ripe. Rotten with age.

The whole place is crumbling round our ears. We need money. D'Eparnelle money. Now do you understand?'

Aliénor stared at the curtain. Her mother's demonstration had been more telling than a thousand words. There had been no noise, no ripping sound. She hadn't pulled at the fabric. It had simply given way.

'But — ' She shook her head. 'But you can sell a property. A house. Or one of the farms. That's what you've done in the past.'

'Fool! Before the war, yes. But now the Germans take our money in taxes. They requisition the produce from our farms. No one is buying.' The briefest of pauses. 'And your father is already using d'Eparnelle money to pay off his debts.'

That was when Aliénor knew it was over. Her shoulders slumped and the air rushed from her lungs as the fight left her. She felt cold and empty, drained of hope. She was trapped. There could be no escape. Like a deer caught in a lamper's torchlight, she stood motionless, frozen. There was no sound in the room apart from her breathing, ragged and uneven. From outside came the murmur of men's voices and Hortense's tinkling laugh.

'They're coming back.' Thérèse spoke in a harsh whisper. 'Henri must never know about this. Do you understand? There are ways of making him think you're a virgin on your wedding night. His parents mustn't find out either. You're not showing yet. We must get you away from here before you do. When is it due?'

'June.' She was trapped. There was no escape. The words were an ugly refrain repeating endlessly inside her head. Her hopes for a bright future with the man she loved had withered and died. She was immeasurably sad. 'Am I allowed to know what plans you're making for me and my baby?' Her voice was brittle, too loud to her ears, as if it were close to cracking under the strain.

'Don't be impertinent. When the

time comes, you'll go into a clinic. There's a new law which says you don't have to give your name. You, the mother, can be totally anonymous. On all the official documents there'll be just an X in place of your name. No one will ever know you've had a child. Your marriage to Henri can go ahead. No one will be any the wiser.'

Aliénor stared at her. 'And my baby?'

'It will — '

'He or she,' Aliénor corrected sharply. Her eyes held her mother's.

Thérèse's lips pursed. 'He or she,' she conceded, 'will be adopted. Now go,' she continued with a return to anger. 'I must think how I'm going to tell your father.'

14

It was decided Aliénor would go and stay with her aunt Sophie, her father's younger sister and the mother of her cousin and childhood friend Joséphine. It was the one positive aspect during a period of mind-numbing misery: some of Aliénor's happiest memories as a girl were of the times she'd spent with Joséphine and her family. The arrangements were made in the week following Hortense and Auguste d'Eparnelle's departure, and on a crisp sunny day in the first week of the new year Aliénor travelled by train with her parents to her aunt's *manoir* south-east of Poitiers. Her parents would stay with her for a few days before making the return journey.

Her father had taken little part in the preparations, leaving everything in his wife's capable hands. Aliénor had been called to his study the morning after Christmas Day. It was Sunday, and the d'Eparnelles and her mother had walked down to the church in the village.

'Is the child's father German?'

'No,' Aliénor replied, and saw relief in her father's face. 'He's English.'

'Ha. Our so-called allies.' Her father's mouth twisted, and there was bitterness in his voice. 'They sank our fleet at Mers-el-Kebir and now they're bombing our towns and cities.'

What could she say? Aliénor shook her head as the tears that came so frequently filled her eyes again.

Her Aunt Sophie's *manoir* was in a remote country area only a few kilometres from what had until just over a year before been the demarcation line between Occupied and Free France. 'Free', Peter had told her, only until the day in November of the previous year when the Germans had decided they needed to bolster their defences along the Mediterranean coast and had sent men in without bothering to consult the Vichy government, even though that government was as fervently pro-Nazi as Hitler himself. Their action had exposed Free France's independence for the farce it was.

As with the Château de la Tour Dragondas, the *manoir* had been commandeered by the Germans at the beginning of the Occupation, and Sophie now lived in the gatehouse. Motherly in a way that Aliénor's own mother had never been, she welcomed her niece with open arms. She'd lost both husband and daughter through illness. Her son had been a captain in the French army, one of the almost two million soldiers taken prisoner in the early months of the war. She hadn't heard from him for more than a year, and feared the worst.

As the days lengthened into spring and summer, the baby quickened and grew. Aliénor often sat by the window of her room, looking out over the forests and fields, hands cradling the growing curve of her stomach. She'd found a kind of peace, although resignation was the better choice of word. Time after time her thoughts went to Peter, and she relived with bittersweet pain their all too short time together, the sadness of her lost love like a heavy weight on her heart. She was resigned to her fate: she would have their baby, would give it up for adoption, would marry Henri. No fairytale ending lay in store, *hélas*.

★   ★   ★

It was a bad time to be giving birth, a dangerous time of apprehension and upheaval. It was on the seventh of June that Aliénor checked into the Clinique du Bon Endroit in Poitiers, under the name Madame Edith X, accompanied by her parents and Aunt Sophie. The staff were agog with the news that a vast force of Allied troops had landed in Normandy the day before. It could only mean one thing: the war would soon be over and France would be free again.

Peter was on his way, Aliénor thought when she heard. Hope flared and she felt his baby kick inside her, sharing her joy. Reality returned the very next moment, dousing her hope: she couldn't keep the baby and she had to marry Henri. There was no escape.

She sat in the armchair by the window of her private room, staring out, conscious of the familiar feeling of resignation that crept over her. Her parents and aunt had gone but would be frequent visitors. They were staying at a nearby hotel. The clinic was close to the station, and the heavy-laden goods trains that rumbled past rattled the window panes.

Excitement fizzed in the air, vying with fear. Bands of resistance fighters, often with weapons provided by the SOE, the Special Operations Executive, attacked groups of German soldiers or sabotaged railway lines. But the German reprisals were barbaric in their ferocity. People were hanged or shot, the innocent as well as the guilty, often at a ratio of ten Frenchmen for every one German. Their high command was sending a clear message. Any defiance would be ruthlessly suppressed.

On the morning of the twelfth, a kind of shocked hush seemed to have settled on Poitiers. Fewer people than normal walked along the street outside the clinic, and the few there were didn't stop to talk to each other.

'What's going on?' Aliénor asked. Her waters had broken, and one of the midwives had come to check that all was well.

'The SS *Das Reich* division is going through Poitiers. They're taking their tanks and half-tracks through. They moved into the southern parts of the city overnight, and they'll carry on through and on towards Normandy tonight.'

'They're *here*?' As if by instinct, Aliénor's hands went round her stomach. 'You heard what happened at Oradour?'

The midwife nodded. Only two days before, soldiers from the SS *Das Reich* division had rounded up the inhabitants of a town not far away called Oradour-sur-Glane. There had been close to seven hundred people, mainly women and children. The soldiers had shot some, pushed others down wells, and burnt the church many had taken shelter in. It had been a brutal unforgivable massacre of innocent people, but Aliénor sensed with a shiver that it wouldn't be the last such massacre before the war was over.

She was restless, knowing her baby would be born before the day's end. Born into a world of fear and danger, she thought, looking out on to the near-empty street as she paced up and down, stretching her spine to ease the contractions.

'You're sure you've found a good home for the baby?' Aliénor stopped her pacing and turned to look at her mother. She and her aunt had come to spend the day with her while her father lingered over a glass of wine and read the papers in the café opposite the station.

Her mother looked up from her needlepoint. 'For the hundredth time, yes. The doctor has found a young professional couple. He hasn't told me any more than that. It's best not to know too much,' she added.

In case I try to make contact, Aliénor thought. Another contraction tugged at her and she crossed to the chest of drawers, touching the neat pile of clothes that lay on top. She'd knitted three of each item, one to wear, one to wash and one to be drying: matinee jackets, rompers, bootees and mittens with ribbon ties, and beribboned bonnets, all in a fine white wool, suitable for either a boy or a girl. Her aunt had been lucky to find the wool and had used up both her own and Aliénor's clothing coupons in the process.

Aliénor asked the doctor the same question when he came to examine her after lunch. She lay on her back on the bed, her hands clasped across the swell of her stomach. The fingers of her right hand twisted round and round the plain gold ring Thérèse had brought from home that now sat on her wedding finger. It would never do, of course, for the clinic to take in an unmarried woman.

'Yes. Be reassured.' The doctor pulled her nightgown back down over her legs. 'Baby will be quite a while yet.' He patted her hands reassuringly. 'The people I've found, they'll love baby as if it were their own.' He glanced across at the little pile of clothes. 'I'll be taking baby straight away,' he warned gently.

Aliénor bit her lip. 'I know.'

The midwives had told her that her long hands and feet practically guaranteed her an easy birth, and so it proved to be.

'A beautiful girl,' the midwife said, placing the tiny shawl-wrapped bundle against Aliénor's breast. They were alone in the room. Her parents and aunt had been asked to wait elsewhere, and the doctor had been called to another patient. It meant she could snatch a few more precious minutes with her baby.

Oh but she was beautiful. So beautiful. Perfect in every way. Aliénor sank back against the pillows, wonder in her eyes and in the smile that curved her lips. Her hair, look at her hair. She touched her fingers to it. So soft, so dark, and so much of it, sticking up in spikes. There was down, like velvet, along the backs of her ears, look. Eyebrows, lashes, that tiny nose and Cupid's-bow mouth.

'Mélisande Petra,' she breathed.

It was quiet in the room. Darkness had fallen — Aliénor's labour had been easy but long, and it was now close to midnight — and the shutters were closed and barred against the clear moonlit sky. She'd asked for the windows to be left open, and the smell of coal from the station opposite drifted in on the warm dust-scented air.

The baby made little snuffling noises, and from time to time her tiny hand moved light as a caress across the skin of Aliénor's chest. So perfect, she thought, and tensed as another contraction caught her.

'Not long now, *madame*,' the midwife said. She meant the afterbirth. Or was it a careless, cruel reminder?

Aliénor frowned as a deep prolonged droning, growing louder with each second, made the walls vibrate. A goods train rumbling through the station? Or were the tanks and half-tracks of the SS division on the move at last? The electric light in the ceiling flickered, and Aliénor looked up in alarm, her hand moving to cover her baby's head.

And suddenly all was noise and confusion. Another contraction, and Aliénor felt the warm mass of the afterbirth slither out. There were noises in the corridor outside, anxious voices, shouts. The ground beneath her bed shook as an endless, rolling explosion thudded down. The ceiling light flickered again. The door burst open. It was the doctor.

No, not yet. Please, God. Not yet.

'*Un raid aérien.*' He pushed a wheelchair into the room. Her parents and aunt followed close behind. 'Help get her and the baby ready, and take them down to the cellars,' he said to the midwife. 'I can't take the baby yet,' he added to her parents before turning and leaving.

Aliénor looked at the anxious faces of those in the room with her. The repeated crump of bombs sounded very close. Each time, the walls of the clinic shook with the impact. 'Quick,' she said, holding her baby to her as she lifted herself upright.

In a matter of minutes, she and her baby were ready. Her father opened the door and wheeled her out into the noisy press of people heading towards the stairs that led down to the cellars. Nurses in white, their head-dresses flowing out behind them, and grim-faced doctors urged patients along. In front of Aliénor, a man on crutches dragged his bandaged leg behind him. A young boy, his arm in a sling, cried as his mother pushed him forward. Voices rose as speculation vied with the explosions outside.

'They're bombing the railway.'

'The SS *Das Reich* division too. I bet you.'

'Hope you're right. Murderers. They deserve everything they get.'

'Don't know how, but the Resistance will have told the Allies they're here in Poitiers tonight.'

'Stupid place to have a clinic. Right by a railway station.'

An explosion came like a thunderclap when the storm is immediately above, punching shockwaves through the air. The walls shook. Aliénor heard a whoomph as masonry collapsed into rubble, and wondered, heart pounding, if part of the clinic had been hit.

The cellars had clearly been used as a

shelter before. Metal tables, brought down from the operating theatres perhaps, lined every wall. Mattresses had been placed underneath. This wasn't the first time Poitiers had been bombed, of course.

Shaky with fear, Aliénor sat on a mattress on the floor and leant back against the wall, hugging her baby close. Her parents and aunt were on each side, the metal table above them protecting them all. The noise from outside was as loud as ever: the constant drone of what she now knew to be Allied aircraft, the thump as bombs exploded, other explosions that she thought might be anti-aircraft fire, the hollow rush as limestone and brick slid to the ground.

It seemed wrong somehow. Profiting from the misfortune of others. People would die that night. She and her family might not live to see the morning. But she pushed any guilt aside. She'd been given a few more precious — what? Minutes? Hours? She didn't know. It didn't matter. She only knew she'd make the most of whatever time she had left with her daughter.

The lights stayed on but the voices around her died away one by one. Other patients, family members, medical personnel all settled down for the night, somehow managing to find a fitful sleep. The air-raid was over, but no one moved from the cellars, just in case. Aliénor heard the occasional footfall as a nurse or doctor did the rounds of their makeshift ward.

She didn't sleep. She was wide awake, in a world of her own, a world that contained only herself and her baby. She held her in her arms, touched her, stroked her, smoothed her fingertips along her eyebrows. Her eyes were deepest blue, just like Peter's.

But the man she loved was lost to her, and she closed her eyes against the pain of it. He would never know the joy of seeing, touching, holding his child. With a sob, she bent her head and buried her face in the folds of the shawl, breathing in the fragrance of her daughter's soft, warm body.

She must have slept. She awoke with a start, her heart beating faster. She brushed the backs of her fingers across her baby's cheek. It was warm, and she breathed a sigh of relief.

The first glimmers of dawn sent pale light through the high cellar windows when she touched her mother's arm, bringing her awake.

'I've come to a decision.' Tears filled her eyes but her voice, low and determined, didn't falter. 'I will *not* have my child adopted. And if you insist on adoption, then I won't marry Henri.'

She heard the sound her mother made, somewhere between a gasp and a hiss, short and sharp. It was probably just as well, she thought, that she couldn't see her mother's face.

'I won't have her adopted,' she repeated. 'We must find some other way.'

15

Aliénor had known there was something wrong with their marriage from the very first night. Well before her wedding day, she'd come to recognise Henri was a less than ardent suitor. She hadn't seen him since that day more than eighteen months before when he'd come down to the Château de la Tour Dragondas with his parents to arrange their marriage. Since then, they'd exchanged little notes and gifts at the turn of the year and on their birthdays, but she sensed that he, like her, acted out of duty rather than affection.

The war was over for most French people. Almost all of the country had been liberated in August and September. General Hartmann and his men had left the château, though no one knew where. It was possible they'd been ordered to join one of the isolated pockets along the Atlantic or Channel coasts where the Germans fought on. Or that they'd gone to France's eastern frontier and the Low Countries where the fighting still raged, more intense than ever.

Things were coming back to normal, but food, wood and coal for the fire and for cooking, and clothing were still in short supply. And so her mother had taken out of its box, wrapped in fine paper, the dress she'd worn in 1919 for her wedding to Aliénor's father, complete with veil, train and elbow-length satin gloves. In creamy lace, the dress itself would have swept the floor when her mother wore it, but barely reached Aliénor's ankles. But the ensemble made her look tall and elegant, and not the least gawky, and she loved it.

'I look like a princess in a fairy tale,' she breathed, forgetting her apprehension for a brief moment. It was the morning of her wedding day, the twenty-fourth of December 1944. Her mother and a maid had just finished helping her get dressed, and she stood in front of the long mirror in her room, looking at her reflection.

Thérèse took her daughter's hand in hers and gave it a squeeze. Rising on tiptoes, she pressed a kiss to her cheek. 'You do indeed, *ma fille.*'

Her mother's gesture was so unexpected, so out of character, that tears came to Aliénor's eyes, and it occurred to her that her mother understood something at least of what she was going through. Her baby, six months old now, lived nearby, cared for by one of Aunt Apolline's granddaughters. The child was thriving, and Aliénor couldn't be other than happy at that. Even so, she grieved for her loss. If only she could have her baby with her.

She grieved too for the loss of the man she loved. He was as dead to her as if he'd died shot down in a hail of German bullets. She closed her eyes against the pain of it. If Peter appeared at the château today, she'd have to turn him away. Nothing must stop her marriage to Henri d'Eparnelle.

The wedding was a civil ceremony, officiated by the mayor of Loudun who arrived just as the icy rain eased off a fraction, and held in the château's *grand salon*. Despite the difficult travelling conditions — so many railway lines had been sabotaged or bombed — all the invited family and friends, together with most of the people who lived on the family estate, had crowded into the large ornately painted room. Aliénor was deeply touched.

Many of the invited guests had arrived a day or two before, and would be staying on a few days more, thanks to d'Eparnelle money which was already pouring into the château, being used to clear out any trace of German occupancy and to redecorate, albeit with the limited materials available. Henri had arrived the evening before, travelling down from Paris with his best man Olivier Papineau, who was his personal assistant and also a rather talented artist, Aliénor remembered.

'Ready, *ma fille*?' her father asked. They stood just outside the *grand salon*. Her hand was resting on her father's forearm. On her other side was her mother, looking lovely in shimmering pale lilac with, pinned to her shoulder, a corsage of tiny fabric violets the exact shade of her eyes.

Aliénor nodded, unable to speak. She was about to commit herself to a future she didn't want. But she squared her shoulders, tilted her chin and lifted her head high. She owed it to her husband-to-be to forget Peter and the love she had for him. She would do her best, she resolved, to make her marriage work.

Her father gave a nod, the richly carved doors were pulled open, and the three of them moved into the *salon*, followed by a flurry of movement as the servants squeezed in behind them.

The best man had been looking round, waiting for them to come in. Aliénor saw him give Henri a nudge and murmur a word or two, and he too looked round and stood up. If the groom's good looks alone were a guarantee of success in marriage, then theirs was unlikely to fail, she thought as, with her parents on either side, she drew nearer to her husband-to-be. Tall and slim, clean-shaven, his light brown hair slicked back from his forehead with just a touch of oil, he wore a grey single-breasted suit, a pale blue shirt and a darker, toning tie the deep blue of his eyes.

'You look lovely,' he murmured when she finally came to a halt beside him.

Aliénor sensed her parents slip away to sit with the d'Eparnelles in the front row. She gave Henri a shy smile from behind her veil. 'So do you.'

At the end of the short official ceremony, Henri lifted her veil with both hands, delicately drawing the lace folds up and over her head.

'Madame d'Eparnelle, may I?' he asked, as he bent forward to touch a feather-light kiss to her lips.

And it was done. The burst of

clapping that greeted his kiss signalled that, for better, for worse, d'Eparnelle and Rochefontaine de Montfort fortunes were tied together forevermore.

The *vin d'honneur* came next. With the departure of the Germans, Aliénor's father had had the false wall in the cellars taken down, and wines, books, paintings and other treasures had been restored to their rightful places, among them a dozen cases of a wine he'd been keeping for just this day. It was a *pétillant* dating from 1926, the year of Aliénor's birth, and it was delicious, its fine bubbles tingling like fairy dust in her nostrils.

Dancing followed. As the short winter's day drew to a close, candles and electric lights were lit, chairs were pushed to the walls, the carpets rolled to one side, and the village band struck up. Aliénor and Henri looked on. He didn't care for dancing, she learnt.

Dinner was for the invited guests only and was served in the formal dining room. Aliénor sat with Henri and both sets of parents at the head of a table seating forty, with several smaller tables on each side, all resplendent with the Rochefontaine de Montforts' finest tableware. The meal was no doubt excellent, but Aliénor scarcely noticed what she was eating, her appetite driven away by the return of a growing apprehension as the hours slid by. This was the easy part. The difficult part was yet to come.

It was gone eleven when Aliénor and her mother got up from the table. Others had left before them, some tired after the long day, some weighted down by an excess of food and drink as they made their way back to the accommodation prepared for them in the north wing.

Her mother helped her take off her wedding clothes, folding them neatly back into their box, while Aliénor slipped over her head the full-length long-sleeved nightdress of fine white cotton her mother had chosen for her. The maid lit scented candles, turned off the electric light and brushed Aliénor's hair so that it hung in waves about her shoulders. A fire burned in the grate, the logs hissing and sizzling whenever raindrops came down the chimney.

Aliénor climbed into bed, swallowing as she looked round her room. Between them they'd created a scene that was warm and inviting and serene, at odds with the apprehension that gnawed inside her.

Thérèse dismissed the maid with a nod, and came over to sit on the edge of Aliénor's bed. For the second time that day, she took her daughter's hand in hers.

'Be careful, Aliénor,' she said, gesturing with a movement of her head to the diamond and sapphire brooch that lay on the bedside cabinet. There was more than a hint of sharp anxiety in her voice. She, and her father too, of course, were party to a deception. As was Aliénor. 'Wrap it in your hanky. Hide it under your pillow.' She squeezed her daughter's hand and stood up. 'You know where I am if you need me. I'll be along to see you in the morning.'

With that, she left and Aliénor was alone. She sat up in the bed, pulling her legs up and clasping her hands round her knees. Only the pitter-patter of raindrops on the shutters, the spluttering hiss of the logs or a distant peal of laughter from the dining room broke the silence.

It was very late. Was Henri still in the dining room? Or was he in the suite of rooms that was the mirror-image of Aliénor's? In the months before their marriage, he'd sent decorators from Paris to transform the rooms that had once been her cousin Joséphine's. No longer a young girl's den, they had been turned into something adult and masculine.

A gust of wind sent a scatter of raindrops against the shutters. And all at once Henri was there in the room with her, as though conjured up by some magician's spell. He stood by the mantelpiece, the light from the flickering candles and the fire casting moving flame-like shadows over his face and the silky full-length dressing gown he wore.

Aliénor's heart was beating an anxious rhythm in her chest. She ran her tongue round dry lips. 'I haven't done this before,' she said, remembering what she'd said to Peter, unable to look Henri in the eye as she told the lie.

'I — I suppose I'm a novice too, in a way.'

She looked across at him, surprised by the uncharacteristic hesitation. Was he naked beneath the dressing gown? she wondered, conscious of the knot of tension that tightened inside her. She laughed uneasily. 'I thought men were supposed to get masses of experience before they married.'

His face seemed to close. 'Really?' There was a cold edge to his voice. His expression was unreadable. 'Well, this one didn't.'

He blew out the candles on the

mantelpiece, his hands going to the belt of his dressing gown. Aliénor slid down between the fine linen sheets, her anxiety growing deeper by the second.

Henri was a dark shadow given gilded highlights by the glow from the fire as he moved over to the bed, letting his dressing gown fall to the floor. Aliénor twisted on to her side to face him, flinching as she smelt strong alcohol, cognac perhaps, on his breath. Normally so abstemious, why did he now feel the need for alcohol?

'Listen.' He touched his fingertips to her arm. 'I've had a long day. I just want to get this over with as quickly as possible.'

Relief washed through her. 'We're both tired,' she murmured.

She hadn't known what to expect, but it wasn't this. Never this. How could two men be so different in the way they made love to a woman? It wasn't that he was rough with her. But there were no soft words, no whispered endearments, no stroking of her hair, no tender pauses to check she was all right. It was all so cold, so clinical, and Aliénor wanted only to cry.

It was soon over, a merciful release.

'Get some sleep,' he said. The mattress shifted as he got up, and she saw the features of his face in the faint light from the fire as he belted his dressing gown. He didn't look happy either. 'I'm going to have a shower.'

She couldn't sleep. She mustn't sleep. Not yet. She lay on her side, knees drawn up to her chest, rigid with shock. She heard the crackle of the fire as a log shifted, the distant click of the interconnecting door, the creaking of the ancient water pipes as taps were turned on.

Now. She had to do it now. Aliénor pushed her hand under the pillow, taking out her mother's brooch inside her handkerchief. She unwrapped it, opened it, and held the long pin in her hand, fingers curled tightly round, so that only the point was visible. Gritting her teeth, she jabbed it into the thumb of her other hand, near the nail, and watched as the blood welled, glistening in the firelight, before she drew her thumb in a line across her inner thigh.

Again. She had to do it again. And once more for the sheet. Another log shifted and light flared, sending flame shadows dancing up the walls of her room. Aliénor looked down and could just make out darker smudges against the pale skin of her inner thigh and on the linen sheet. It looked authentic, she thought, pushing brooch and handkerchief back under her pillow. Her face crumpled as she remembered her first time, how Peter had gently washed the proof of her virginity away with water from the spring. The tears came then, wrenching sobs for love that was lost and would never be regained.

'Perhaps Hortense was telling the truth when she said he was keeping himself pure for his bride,' Thérèse said, voice slow with speculation. It was the next morning, and Aliénor had told her mother everything that had happened.

Henri hadn't returned during the night. The ruse with the brooch hadn't been necessary after all. 'It could simply be he's just very inexperienced,' she continued with a reassuring smile. But her expression was troubled, and she clearly shared her daughter's unease.

* * *

Aliénor lifted her large breakfast cup in both hands. It held real coffee, not the chicory root substitute they'd all grown so used to. Henri's parents had brought a packet down with them from Paris. They'd arrived the afternoon before and would be staying for the week, leaving just after Easter.

Real coffee, but the effect was the same. Nausea swirled in Aliénor's stomach, and she put the cup down, pushing it away from her. It was the third day running it had had that effect on her. And her breasts were taut and heavy. The signs were there, but she hardly dared hope. If she were right, it could put an end to the misery and despair and endless self-questioning of the previous three months.

She'd wait a week or so, she decided, until she knew for sure. Then she'd tell Henri. He'd be both pleased and relieved.

A small sound made her look up, and she realised with dismay that both her mother and mother-in-law, sitting opposite her, had seen her push her cup away.

'The young things have been busy, I think, Thérèse,' Hortense commented archly.

Thérèse's lips thinned and she sent her daughter a sympathetic look before turning to her sister-in-law, mouth curving into a gracious smile. 'I expect Vincent and Auguste will spend most of the morning in the wine cellars, Hortense.' The two men had had an early breakfast and were now taking advantage of the late-March sunshine to inspect the kitchen gardens. 'So why don't we go into Loudun this morning? It's Tuesday, market day.' The two women fell into a discussion of shopping and shortages, as Thérèse had no doubt known they would, and Aliénor was grateful to her for diverting Hortense's attention. After that first night, when she'd told her mother everything that had happened, Aliénor had been too ashamed to confide too much, but knew her mother was well aware that the situation had not improved.

That first night had set the pattern for those that followed. For Henri it meant a quick five minutes in the marital bed, a shower that set the water pipes creaking for far longer, and sleep in his own bed. Or so she supposed. He certainly never came back to hers. For her it was a cold clinical coupling that left her sobbing into her pillow with worry and frustration. What was wrong? Was she so unattractive? What she'd shared with Peter was worlds away from this. Beyond compare. And it occurred to her that if she'd never experienced Peter's lovemaking, she might never have known what she was missing. Where was he now? she wondered. The war raged on in Germany. Was he there, in the thick of it? Only the other day they'd heard a rumour that a bridge had collapsed at a place called Remagen. Had that been his doing?

On the fourth night, she put her hand on Henri's shoulder, stroking her fingertips lightly down his arm.

'Don't do that.' Henri's voice came to her through the near darkness.

'But I want to.' Her tone was soft, inviting. 'Your skin is warm and smooth, Henri. Please let me touch it.'

'I'd rather you didn't.'

Another night, and her hands went to his waist, gently holding him away.

'Could we make it last a little longer, Henri?' she asked.

'I think not.' In the faint glow from the fire, she could just make out the tense lines of his face. He looked determined. Driven, but not by pleasure, and she knew he was as unhappy as she was.

With a ragged sigh, Aliénor took a slice of toast and spread some jam over it. She had no appetite but forced herself to take a bite, and let the murmur of Thérèse and Hortense's voices wash over her. She didn't understand. He appeared to act out of a grim duty, wanting only to get the whole ordeal over and done with as fast as possible. She came to welcome the times, thankfully quite frequent, when work took him and his personal assistant up to the Paris office or the factories in Saint Velérien, for it gave her a few days' respite.

'What's the problem, Henri? What am I doing wrong? Tell me. Please.' Another loveless coupling had just come to an end and Aliénor pulled herself up into a sitting position in the bed, drawing her knees up to her chest and tugging her nightdress down to her ankles.

Henri had already got out of her bed. He stood with his back to her, burnished shades of gold in the firelight. The body she wasn't allowed to touch, she thought as he pulled on his dressing gown, belting it and turning to look at her. She didn't love him, but she wanted to do all she could to make a success of their marriage.

A log settled, sending a flare of light into the room. His face had that shuttered look she'd come to know so well, the look that made it clear to her there was nothing to discuss. 'Henri, please. I need to know what I can change. I need some answers.' How desperately she needed some answers.

'Look, there's a lot of pressure on me.' His voice held a harsh, angry edge. 'Things will be different once you're with child.'

Aliénor gasped, incredulous. 'Is that what all this is about? Producing an heir to the d'Eparnelle millions? There's more to married life than that, Henri.'

She saw him flinch. 'There's clearly no point in discussing the matter any further. Goodnight, Aliénor.'

As she had so many times before, she

watched him go. Then she turned on to her side and curled herself into a ball, burying her face in the pillow to muffle her crying as the water pipes creaked into life.

Was it true? she asked herself now as she recalled the exchange. Would everything really be different — better — when she was with child? She pushed her plate with its half-eaten slice of toast away and stood up. She hoped so. How very much she hoped so.

Both older women stopped talking and looked at her as she got to her feet. She managed a smile. 'I was thinking about Henri,' she said, and almost sat down again in shock as a memory of Ernst Ostermeyer came unbidden to her mind. The Gestapo colonel had been convinced that Henri would never make her happy. She shivered as though a chill wind blew over her. What had he known that she didn't?

★   ★   ★

'You're expecting a baby? That's marvellous news, Aliénor.' It was a spring evening a fortnight later, and the two of them were walking in the grounds. 'When is it due?'

Aliénor laughed. Henri sounded both pleased and relieved. 'Some time around Christmas,' she said happily.

They continued on in silence, coming to a halt by the edge of the lake. The sky, fiery red with the last rays of the setting sun, was reflected in the still surface of the water.

Henri lifted each of his hands in turn, curling his fingers into his palms to check his nails. 'We mustn't do anything to jeopardise the baby's development.' His tone was carefully neutral.

'No. Of course not,' Aliénor agreed with a frown. She looked out across the water. 'What are you trying to say, Henri?'

He turned to look at her. 'I think it best if we don't — enjoy marital relations for a while.'

'Oh.' A light, uneasy drift of wind played across her skin. Colour crept over her face. She was at a loss for words. Was that what people usually did? It hadn't been an issue during her first pregnancy, of course. She didn't want to harm her baby, that went without saying. And their couplings so far had brought no joy to either of them. But all at once her determination to make a success of their marriage seemed to recede into the distance.

She found her voice at last. 'If that's what you feel best, Henri.'

'It is.'

★ ★ ★

The armistice was signed on the eighth of May, and the war was officially over in Europe, although great armies still fought on in the Pacific. It was a time of rejoicing, but joy was muted by an underlying disquiet. Men who had been prisoners of war for five long years were finally coming home, those who had survived of course. Deportees too, and those who had been sent to Germany as part of the compulsory work programme. Close to two million men, and a smaller number of women, would be returning to their homes. Would they all be able to settle back into their old lives? Or would they find that circumstances had changed and their old lives were no longer an option?

There were other dangers too: unexploded bombs, and buildings weakened by bombing that suddenly collapsed.

'It's an anxious time for a lot of people,' Aliénor said. It was the end of May, and she was in the village, sitting at the table that stood in the centre of Aunt Apolline's large kitchen. Henri and his personal assistant were away for the week. They intended spending two days in Paris and the rest of the time in Saint Velérien. She frowned. There were times when the closeness between the two men made her uneasy.

'You're right, my dear,' Aunt Apolline

was saying. 'There'll be so-called punishments meted out. A lot of settling of old scores too. Just like after Liberation.' The old woman stood by the fireplace, a cloth in her hand, about to lift the hot coffee pot from its hook above the fire. Pea soup bubbled in another pot, mingling its delicate fragrance with the smell of roasted chicory. 'Coffee?'

Aliénor shook her head. It was almost lunch time, but she wouldn't stay. She'd simply popped in on Apolline on her way back to the château. Taking advantage of Henri's absence, she'd cycled earlier that morning to the remote farmhouse where Apolline's granddaughter Florence cared for Aliénor's baby as well as her own children. There, as she often did, she'd spent several hours holding her daughter in her arms, chanting nursery rhymes, and singing lullabies. It was always a bittersweet time that brought an ache to her throat. But her child was thriving, and that was the main thing.

The wise woman came over, stirring the pale greenish contents of a glass which she set down on the table in front of her. 'Stinging-nettle tisane. Full of goodness for someone in your condition.'

Aliénor couldn't help smiling. The old woman didn't miss a thing. 'Thank you.' She sipped it. It was lukewarm and rather unpleasant. 'I saw Suzanne earlier this morning,' she said as Aunt Apolline sat down opposite her. 'She's petrified.'

'That husband of hers was a nasty piece of work. That's one man I'd be glad to see *not* come back.'

Later, as she cycled back home, her thoughts went to Christian. When — if — he came back from the work camp in Germany, how would his life turn out? Would he be able to resume the studies he had so set his heart on? Or would he have to settle for second best, a mind-numbing job somewhere that had no use for his brain?

And what of Ralf? Had he survived the brutal battles fought over every metre of land as the Allied troops tried to push the Germans out? Had he been one of those who had held out till the very end of the war, when most of France had been liberated months before, in the pockets of German resistance along the Atlantic wall? Or had he been lucky enough to reach his home, that town east of Berlin that he'd spoken of so fondly?

And of course Peter, who was never far from her thoughts. Had he come through the war? Where was he now? What was he doing? The sobs came suddenly and she brought her bicycle to a halt, putting unsteady feet on the ground. She bowed her head to the handlebars as, once again, she grieved for what she'd lost. For in all probability, she knew, she would never see him again; would never have any answer to her questions.

16

'Here's a letter from someone who doesn't know you're married.' Aliénor's father passed a cream envelope across the breakfast table to Aliénor and sat down opposite her, next to his wife, ready to tackle his own pile of letters.

Was it prescience of some kind that made her pulses race? She looked at the front of the envelope even as her fingers slipped into the gap between the flap and the back, tearing it open, too impatient to wait until her father had finished with the ivory paper knife. French stamps. M-A-U. She could make out the first three letters of the postmark but no more. Maubeuge? Mauléon? It didn't matter. With fingers that fumbled, she took out the letter, a single sheet of paper folded in two, and unfolded it, eyes going straight to the signature. A laugh of pure happiness came bubbling up. Peter was alive and in France, and he'd written to her. She read the letter. It was short, just two lines. Even so, she couldn't take it in and had to read it again.

My dearest Mélisande
I'll be at the grape-pickers' hut all day Thursday the 7th. Please be there if you can.
Peter

'Something interesting?' her mother enquired, carefully casual as she spread a thin film of jam over her toast, and Aliénor knew the wild burst of excitement that fizzed through her had to be more than visible on her face and in the hands that shook as she put the note back in its envelope. She didn't care. Peter had written. Her darling Peter had written.

'It's from my daughter's father. He wants to see me.'

There was a moment of total stillness. If Aliénor had set out to shock, she had succeeded. Neither of her parents moved. Neither spoke. The only sound was the song of a chaffinch that filtered in through the open windows.

Her father set down the cup of coffee he was holding. 'Are you going to see him?' he asked, his tone neutral.

'Yes.'

Her mother stirred. 'When? And where?' she asked, ever practical.

'The day after tomorrow.' Aliénor saw her parents exchange a look and knew what it meant: relief that Henri wouldn't be there. He and his personal assistant had left the day before to inspect the factories in St Velérien. They weren't due back until Friday. 'He wants to meet me at — ' Her voice faltered. ' — at the place where we used to meet.' All at once it hurt to speak any more. It was a place that held so many precious memories. She hadn't been back at all in the months since Peter had left.

Her father picked his cup up, then set it down again. It was the only visible sign of his unease. 'You are a married woman now.'

Aliénor looked down at her plate as the pleasure the letter had brought faded. She didn't feel married. Now that her pregnancy had been confirmed, Henri came down to the château perhaps two weeks in every four, no more. Although they spent time together, he never held her hand or put his arm round her, and made it clear, when she tried to do so, that he didn't welcome the contact. He no longer graced the marital bed either.

With a sigh, Aliénor now looked up from her plate and gave her father a bleak smile. 'Trust me, *père*, to do what's right.'

Two days later, soon after breakfast, she set off, taking the route she'd taken so many times before through the château grounds, over the gap-toothed wall and up into the long slopes of forest and fields. There was a knot in her chest that wouldn't ease. The euphoria of hearing from Peter had worn off and she'd cried herself to sleep two nights running, for this could never, of course, be the joyous, blissful reunion of her first wild imaginings. As her father had reminded her, she was a married woman now. She had duties, responsibilities.

Peter didn't know she was married. She had to tell him. She had — somehow — to find the words to tell him about the daughter she had borne — their daughter. The first anniversary of her birth was almost upon her. And lastly, she had to say *adieu*. So short a word yet filled with such final, heartbreaking meaning: 'Goodbye, my love, you are lost to me forever.'

She pulled off the straw hat that protected her face from the June sunshine, wiping her cheeks with the heel of her hand before putting it back on her head. She was almost there. Soon, it would all be over.

It was almost two years since she'd last been to this place, but the hut had scarcely changed. She stood some fifty metres away, keeping to the shadows of the forest, reluctant to go any further, reluctant to do what she had to do. The vines were more neglected than ever, last year's long stems climbing up though there was nothing to climb against, swaying in the breeze.

The door to the hut opened. And there he was, his tall lean body and dark hair unmistakable as he ducked under the lintel. His eyes went straight to her. Even from this distance, she could see the happiness that lit up his face as he came towards her, first walking then breaking into a run.

'Peter,' she breathed.

And she was running to meet him, slammed into him, and his hands went low to her waist, her arms went round his neck, and he was squashing her against his chest and lifting her up, swinging her round, and it was glorious. She was laughing and crying, calling his name, murmuring words of endearment. She'd lost her hat at some point but she didn't care.

'Mélisande, my sweetheart. I can't believe you're here.' His voice was gruff as he set her down again, his hands at her waist still, pulling her hard in against him. 'I thought I'd never see you again.'

'The war's over, Peter. I don't have a code name anymore. Call me by my real name. Aliénor.' She leant against him, desire flaring, fierce and sweet. 'Kiss me, Peter.'

And she gave herself over to the intensity of his lips on hers, the heat of his body against hers, the strength in the arms that held her. One part of her knew it couldn't — it mustn't — last. But she couldn't help it. She couldn't stop. Not just yet. She was greedy for his touch.

She pulled away, cupping his face in both hands, fingertips tangling in the hair at his temples. A smile curved her lips as her eyes met his. 'You're looking thin, my love. And pale.'

His arms stroked up and down her back. 'I was a prisoner in Germany for the last six months of the war. We ate nothing but cabbage soup and whatever we could scrounge.'

'They caught you?' Aliénor's thoughts flashed back to the night she'd spent at the Pierre Levée prison in Poitiers, the dreadful cries and shouts and moans she'd heard, and her blood ran cold. 'Did they torture you?'

He shook his head. 'Nothing like that. They didn't realise who exactly they'd caught. If they had, they'd have hanged me.'

'Tell me.' His hair, untamed by water, oil or comb, shone in the sunlight. She couldn't stop looking at him, touching him. And he was the same. His deep blue eyes never left hers. 'No,' she corrected herself. 'Tell me everything you've done since — since the September you went back to England.' She let the fingers of both hands trail down his face, loving the rasp of his jaw against the soft pads of her thumbs.

'Everything? My sweet Aliénor, you don't ask much, do you?' He took both her hands in his, started to brush a kiss across each fingertip in turn.

All at once he stilled. For the briefest of seconds he held her hand, her left hand, motionless to his lips, and she knew he'd touched her wedding ring. Something like pain crossed his face.

'Not yet, Peter.' There was desperation in her voice. 'Let's not talk about it yet.'

Abruptly he swung away, pushing taut fingers through his hair. Her arms fell to her sides, and the warmth of his body was replaced by the chill of loss. He turned back, his eyes holding hers. 'Soon,' he said, his voice a growl.

'Yes,' she promised, all too aware that something precious had gone from his gaze.

'Let's walk over to the hut.'

They walked side by side, not touching, and the breeze that had been so pleasant now blew cool breaths across her skin.

Peter pushed his hands into the pockets of his trousers. 'They sent me back to France at the end of October '43, this time to Lille.' His mission, he told her, was essentially the same as it had been before, to make contact with local resistance groups and to train people in the use of explosives to blow up railway tracks, power lines, and any other target that presented itself.

He told his tale simply, the odd flash of humour a small light amid the horror of those harrowing times when he'd worked in the shadows of the night, fear of capture his constant companion. But there was anger in his voice, and Aliénor knew it had everything to do with the present and nothing to do with the events he was recounting. Her heart ached, for him and for herself.

They reached the hut and sat down on the bench that ran along the outside wall, side by side still, not touching. It was as if an unbridgeable gulf separated them. Perhaps it was for the best, Aliénor thought, blinking back the tears that came too often now.

'Tell me how you got arrested,' she said, voice husky with emotion.

Peter looked out over the rows of vines and beyond, and she wondered how much he saw. 'I was on a train going back to Lille. The compartment was empty apart from me, a man sitting over by the window, and a girl opposite him. She was fifteen, sixteen at most.' His voice took on a hard edge. 'The man leant across and slid his hand along her thigh under her skirt. The poor girl didn't know how to handle it. So I asked him to stop and when he didn't, I punched him. Twice.' His smile was grim. 'Gave him a bloody nose and a bruised jaw. The so-and-so deserved every bit of it. Unfortunately, he called the guards and had me arrested.'

'Oh Peter.' She was both shocked and proud. She sat with her hands in her lap and longed to reach across and touch him, but she didn't. It was for the best, she told herself again.

Able-bodied but with no job, he was

plainly a shirker, he went on, and was deported to Germany, a mistake on the Germans' part because the storage area of the munitions factory where he was sent to work blew up shortly after his arrival. The locomotive yard he was sent to next fared no better, though in a different way, with productivity in decline and machines that kept breaking down.

Aliénor smiled, imagining the chaos he'd created, knowing he was clever and subtle enough not to be found out.

'Those last months of the war in Germany were bad. There was never enough food. From time to time you could get rabbit. Strangely, though, they always came with their ears cut off.'

She frowned, not understanding.

Another grim smile. 'They were cats, skinned, gutted and ready to cook.'

Her stomach turned. 'Oh Peter. What you must have gone through.'

'I'm alive. Millions weren't so lucky.' He fell silent, looking out across the vines to the forest beyond. 'So.' He drew his shoulders back and turned to look at her. 'You married him. You couldn't wait.' The accusation stung, sharp as a slap, and Aliénor felt colour sweep into her face.

'I could never have married you, Peter. People in my family don't marry for love.'

He flinched. His eyes, over-bright, looked at something far away. At last he spoke. 'Are you happy with him?'

'No.' She lowered her gaze to the hands that twisted in her lap.

'Then leave him. Come to England with me.'

Oh how easy it would be to yield to that temptation. Excitement flooded through her.

But it wasn't as simple as that. She had resolved to do everything she could to make her marriage to Henri work. And the cruel truth was her parents were relying on his family's money.

She swallowed. 'I'm carrying his child.'

All expression left his face. He turned

his head away to look out over the vines again, and leant back against the wall. 'I see.'

Aliénor hesitated. 'There's more.' Her voice shook. 'I had a baby. Your baby. A little girl.'

'Your husband has agreed to have another man's bastard in his house?'

She gasped. The brutal words, aiming to shock, stabbed into her. 'No. He doesn't know.'

He frowned. 'So where is she now?'

'She's being looked after by someone who lives not too far away. She's thriving, Peter.'

'Why didn't you tell me about her?'

'How could I?'

'You'll have to explain.' His anger blazed at her, and each word that came at her was a fresh stab of the knife. 'Tell me everything.'

So she told him how she and Christian had been arrested as they left the airfield, and about her release and Christian's deportation.

'He was my only contact with the

Resistance. That's how it was organised. There was no one else I knew who could get a message through to you.'

'If only — ' He pushed a hand over the top of his head and down, fingers digging in hard at the nape. His anger was directed at himself now. 'I should have given you my grandmother's address in Switzerland. God dammit.' He heaved in a breath. 'Tell me the rest.'

She told him that it had been essential no one find out about her pregnancy, otherwise her marriage to Henri couldn't have gone ahead, how she'd gone to stay with her aunt, how she'd used the name Edith X at the clinic in Poitiers, and how she'd given birth anonymously because there could be no record to link her with the birth of an illegitimate baby.

'My parents wanted her to be adopted. But I couldn't let them do that. She doesn't know I'm her mother. She'll be brought up to think I'm just a friend of the family. Henri must never find out that she exists.'

For a long moment he stared at her, his mouth working in a parody of a smile, full of pain.

'Tell me I'm dreaming. Tell me this nightmare is a dream.' He twisted away, turning his back on her and standing up in one swift movement. He stood there, back ramrod straight, revealing nothing. Then he walked off, round the hut, out of sight.

Aliénor waited, shaken, knowing he needed time by himself. Birdsong, holding all the promise of early summer, came to her from the nearby trees and all at once she couldn't wait any longer, couldn't let him suffer alone.

She found him the other side of the hut, and stopped dead, a metre away. He stood facing the wall, leaning his forehead into the arm he held against the rough stones. With the bunched fist of his other hand he hit the wall, once, twice, with such force that pieces of mortar and stone fell to the ground.

He'd heard her coming. 'Tell me her name. My daughter's name.' He didn't turn round. He didn't move from where he was.

'Mélisande Petra. It's her birthday next Tuesday. The twelfth of June. She'll be one year old.'

His fist thudded into the wall again and more fragments fell. She saw him draw in a long shuddering breath and wipe his face just once across the sleeve of his shirt before he turned to look at her.

His smile was bleak, not really a smile at all. 'So I've lost you — and the daughter I never knew I had, both in one day.'

It was more than she could bear. She reached up to touch fingertips to his cheek. His skin was damp. 'I'm sorry, Peter. I'm so sorry.'

'Just once. I want to see my daughter just once. Tell me how to get there. I've hired a car. It's down in the village.'

She gave him the directions in a voice that shook.

'Let me kiss you one last time,' he said.

She could only nod.

His kiss was gentle, achingly tender, of such sweet intensity that tears spilled down her face. It was an unbearable farewell and she pulled away, stumbling. 'I must go now.'

Somehow she found the strength to walk away. But after only a few metres, she had to look back. He stood there still, motionless, and there were tears in his eyes too.

'*Adieu.*' The word was little more than a broken whisper, choking in her throat. '*Adieu*, my sweet love.' And she turned away, knowing she would never see him again.

17

She headed for the spring, of course. She needed the soothing peace that secret place always brought.

Blindly, eyes misted by tears, she pushed into the untamed part of the wood. Brambles tugged at her clothes. She jumped, heartbeat jolting, then stood totally still as boar piglets ran squealing, crashing unseen through the undergrowth. The mouth-watering scent of wild strawberries made her stop again, and she crouched to pick the small red fruit tucked away between dark leaves.

At last she reached the spring. Bright rods of sunlight pierced the canopy of branches to fall on the woodland floor and the trickle of water that flowed lazily across it. Stepping carefully over the slippery stones, she came to the point where the water welled up. Here she knelt, letting the strawberries roll off her palm on to the rock, a tasty offering to the ancient gods.

But for once, the quiet beauty of the place failed to work its healing magic. The dark ivy that fell like a curtain on to the woodland floor, the murmur of the water, the rich earthy smell all brought back too-vivid images of that long afternoon when she'd lain here in Peter's arms.

Pain swelled in her throat. Peter. The man she loved. The man she could never call her own.

Restlessly, she moved off again, taking the path that would bring her to the château. When she'd told Peter that people in her family didn't marry for love, she'd spoken simple truth. But her heart protested against the emotional emptiness that lay where laughter and loving, caring and concern should have been. She knew what it was to love and be loved. Was it so wrong to want something approaching that in her marriage?

Divorce, or even a separation, was out of the question. Her family's fortunes were too closely tied to Henri's. Thanks to him and his family's money, her parents were free of debt, restoration work had started on the château and its grounds, there were jobs on the estate for everyone who needed one, and a new factory was being built nearby. Like little Mélisande, the whole area was thriving. Surely, she thought, bitter tears stinging her eyes, surely her happiness, or rather unhappiness, was a small price to pay.

She cuffed the tears away as she drew nearer the château. Coming out of the trees, she started crossing the lawn, making for the terrace. She heard a car roar into life, and looked up to glimpse the rounded lines of a black car disappearing at speed down the drive towards the gatehouse.

A moment's unease broke into her misery. The gendarmes? Why had they come to the château? She hurried up the steps, crossed the terrace and let herself into the hall.

She'd come into the hall the back way. At the other end of the room — the front of the château — one of the maids was closing the huge double doors on the visitors who had just left. Aliénor frowned, unease turning to alarm as the maid wiped a handkerchief across each eye in turn. Small sounds of distress, like the whimpering of a puppy, escaped her.

'What is it, Brigitte? What's wrong?' Aliénor cried, running over to her.

'Oh, *madame*. Dreadful news — ' She stopped, pressing the handkerchief to her mouth. '*Monsieur* Henri — '

Aliénor's heart missed a beat. 'What's happened? Is he all right?'

The maid's tears began again. 'You must go to your father, *madame*. He's in his study.'

Frightened now, Aliénor gave the maid's shoulder a brief squeeze. 'Go and rest a while, Brigitte.' And she was off, running, heart pounding, along the gallery to her father's study.

He was on the phone. He looked up as she burst in and held his hand up, warning her not to interrupt. 'Ah, she's here now.' His tone was sombre.

Her mother stood by the window, looking out. She glanced round when Aliénor came in, then turned back, looking out over the grounds again.

' . . . Yes, Auguste . . . ' her father was saying. 'At least, with the baby due at Christmas, he's assured the succession . . . '

'The estate will stay in the family, thank goodness,' Thérèse murmured.

Aliénor looked from one parent to the other. 'What's going on? Tell me.' There was an edge of panic in her voice.

' . . . Yes . . . ghastly.'

Her father put the phone down, stood up and walked round to his daughter. 'I'm afraid I've got bad news, *ma fille*,' he said, bringing his hands up to grip her upper arms. 'Henri is dead.'

'Dead? No.' She shook her head, mind recoiling.

'A bomb.' Her father spoke gently. 'An unexploded bomb. Near the factory at St Velérien. He and his assistant and four others were killed.'

'No.' A sob choked in her throat. Was it her imagination, or did Henri's unborn child move inside her, as shaken as she was, perhaps? She shook her head again. 'No.'

'It would have been instant, *ma fille*.'

'Instant?' The tears came then, spilling down her cheeks, unstoppable. All at once she was overwhelmed with grief at the senseless waste of it, the loss of a young life that had held so much promise. Grief too for what might have been. She hadn't loved Henri and he hadn't loved her, but they could perhaps have made a go of their marriage. He'd loved the château, its history, its architecture. In his cool, efficient way he'd been a very successful businessman. And, she sensed, he would have been a good father to their child.

She became aware that her father was

patting her arm. His other hand had fallen to his side. He looked uncomfortable, as though embarrassed by the show of emotion. Her mother stood by the window still.

Suddenly, it was more than she could bear. She pushed the heel of her hand across her face, wiping away the tears.

'I must go. I'll need the car. And Bertrand.' Her voice was breathless, shaky.

She heard Thérèse's sharp 'Where are you going?' but she didn't answer. Already she was turning, heading out, running towards the north wing where she found Bertrand, the chauffeur, polishing the family's pre-war Citroën.

Moments later, they were on their way. *Please, God, let me be in time*, she thought, sending another prayer heavenward because obtaining petrol was no longer a problem now the war was over. Cycling there would have taken far too much time.

Hurry, hurry. And her mind went back to that frantic cycle ride up to the grape-pickers' hut the day she'd found out Peter was flying back to England. Then, she'd been in time. And now?

Florence and her family lived in a farmhouse as isolated as Suzanne's, but in the opposite direction and much further away.

'Faster, Bertrand,' Aliénor urged as the car bumped and swayed along the narrow country roads. She sat forward, taut and anxious, pulse racing. 'Go faster.'

At last they reached the lane that led to Florence's house. The chauffeur swung round the bend, and Aliénor's heart leapt. A new-looking Renault was parked tucked close in to the high stone wall. It had to be the car Peter had hired. He was still there.

Bertrand pulled to a halt. She jumped out and ran to the side gate. She pushed it open and her heart leapt again. There he was.

He stood in the middle of the courtyard, holding his daughter in his arms. By his side was Florence, holding the hand of one of her children. Her other child was hop-skip-and-jumping nearby.

In the moment she stood in the gateway, Aliénor took it all in — the gleam of sunlight on his thick, dark hair, the smiling laugh on his beautiful face, little Mélisande's squeals of delight. Joy at the sight brought an ache to her throat. Father and daughter looked so natural together, so happy and at ease. So perfect.

She saw Florence's mouth move; couldn't hear what she said. Then Peter was looking in her direction. He must have seen something in her face, because straight away he handed his daughter to Florence, and started running towards her. And she too was running, tears streaming down her face. 'Oh Peter — '

His arms came round her and he swept her into his embrace. 'Hush, my sweet. Don't cry.' Gently, he drew her head against his shoulder, pressing kisses to her hair.

'It's Henri.' The words came in raggedy sobs. 'He's dead. A bomb blew up.'

The movement of his lips on her hair, his hands on her back, stilled for an instant. 'Aliénor, my dear . . . ' He picked her up effortlessly, as though she weighed no more than a child, and carried her across to the bench outside the kitchen door. She barely registered Florence taking the children inside the house; barely heard the soft click as the other woman closed the door behind her.

Peter, her Peter. How she welcomed his warmth, his strength. He was holding her, rocking her, cradling her in his arms. He murmured soothing words, and let her speak her grief and anger, her regret and her guilt. 'I tried, Peter. I tried. I wanted our marriage to work. But . . . '

She fell silent at last.

'This is far too soon,' Peter said, stroking her hair. 'I'll ask you again after a decent interval.'

Aliénor's heart skipped a beat. She lifted her head. 'Ask me what, Peter?'

'You, me, little Mélisande.' He placed the flat of his palm across her stomach. 'And Henri's child in there . . . we're a ready-made family.' He paused, and Aliénor could see his eyes were over-bright. 'Will you marry me, Aliénor?'

Tears filled her eyes. She brought her hand up, touching her fingers to the strong line of his jaw. 'Yes, Peter. It's what I want more than anything in the world. Yes.'